W9-AMT-770

James M. Cain Titles Available in Vintage

LOVE'S LOVELY COUNTERFEIT

James M. Cain

LOVE'S LOVELY COUNTERFEIT

VINTAGE BOOKS
A Division of Random House
New York

FIRST VINTAGE BOOKS EDITION, October 1979

Copyright 1942 and renewed 1970 by James M. Cain

Library of Congress Cataloging in Publication Data

Cain, James Mallahan, 1892–1977.
  Love's lovely counterfeit.

  Reprint of the 1945 ed. published by World Pub., Cleveland.
  I. Title.
PZ3.C11993Lo 1979   [PS3505.A3113]   813'.5'2
79-10778
ISBN 0-394-74213-3

Manufactured in the United States of America

Cover photo: Ron Tunison

LOVE'S LOVELY
COUNTERFEIT

I

Through the revolving door came a tall man with big shoulders, who crossed to the elevators, and after nodding to the starter, stood looking over the lobby. It was the standard lobby, for hotels of the first class in cities of the second class, to be found all over the United States: it had quiet, comfortable furniture; illuminated signs with green letters over the windows of grand functionaries; oil paintings of lakes, streams, and forests; and heavy urns, filled with sand, for cigarettes. Various desks, tables, and booths, staffed with women in assorted uniforms, gave it a touch of high, wartime consecration. Yet, in spite of all this, it contrived to seem a bit disreputable. Possibly the clientele, now debouching from dining room, fountain room, and cocktail bar, grabbing its hats after lunch, and hastening away, had something to do with this. It was made up of men distinctly political, together with the slightly too good-looking women one encounters behind desks in city halls. Indeed, many of them, after leaving the hotel, streamed over to the City Hall across the street, a traffic cop blowing his whistle as each batch appeared, and making this rite seem portentous, as though the vehicles that he stopped had all the panting impatience of an Empire State Express.

The man at the elevators, however, noted little of this, and seemed so much a part of it that he may have been incapable of seeing it. He was at least six feet, and something about his carriage suggested that at some time in his life he had been a professional athlete. His face, however, was at variance with the rest of him. Although he was not far from thirty, it had a juvenile look, and the part that was face, as distinguished from the parts that were cheek, jowl, and chin, seemed curiously small. Allowing for that, he had a fair amount of masculine good looks. His hair was light, with the tawniness that touches such hair in the late twenties. His eyes were blue, his skin showed the sunburn of many seasons; his step, as he entered the car, was springy. He rode up to the seventh floor, got out, walked down a corridor, stopped before a door with no number on it, pressed a button. A slot opened, then the door opened, and he went in.

The room he entered was large, with the usual hotel furniture and a grand piano that was enameled in green and pointed in gold. He gave a wipe at this as he went by, so the keys made a startled clatter, and went on to an office that adjoined the big room. Seated at a desk here was the owner of the hotel, Mr. Sol Caspar, who had no share of masculine good looks or any other kind of good looks. He was a short, squatty man in his middle thirties, and although it was a warm day in May, and the people in the lobby had been wearing straw hats, he was dressed in a heavy brown suit, with handkerchief to match and custom-made shoes. There was a six-pointed star on his ring and a mazuza on the door-casing, but these were caprices, or possibly affectations for business reasons. Actually he had no Hebraic connections, for his real name was Salvatore Gasparro, and no doubt it was his origin that prompted him to name his hotel for Columbus, a popular hero with Italo-Americans. He was playing solitaire with his hat on the back of his head, and didn't look up when the other man came in and sat down. Nor did he look up a few minutes later, when a bellboy appeared, set a package on the desk, opened it, and tiptoed out. Soon, however, he put the cards away and gave his attention to the package. It was an album of records, and he put them on a phonograph that stood against the wall behind him. Then he snapped a button, sat at his desk, lit a cigar, and took off his hat. They were of the opera *Il Trovatore,* and evidently met with his approval. When the tenor sang an aria full of high notes he played it over, then played it over again. But when a minor tenor started a slow recitative he became bored, and stopped the machine.

Only then did he greet his visitor, who had sat staring straight in front of him, obviously not entertained by the music. In a rough, high voice, though without any trace of accent, he said: "H'y, Benny."

"Hello, Sol."

"How they treating you?"

"O.K. so far."

"They got you in the draft yet?"

"No, I still got my football hernia."

"Oh that's right. What you got on tonight?"

"I guess you forgot. This is my day off."

"I said what you got on?"

". . . Nothing I can think of now. Why?"

"Little job."

"What kind of a job?"

"Don't take it like that, Benny. You ought to know by now I don't call on you for any rough stuff. This is nothing to be worried about. Political meeting."

"And what's that?"

"Where the voters get together and pick out who's not going to be elected. Or so I hear. I never been to one."

"And where do I come in?"

"You look it over."

"I still don't get it."

"They got a Swede that's running for mayor. A lug that says he's out to get me. It's about time I found out what he's up to."

"You mean this milkman, Jansen?"

"That's him."

"How would I know what he's up to?"

"Maybe you don't get all the fine points, but you can see who's there. That's the main idea."

"I don't know any of these birds."

Mr. Caspar's eyes were the most arresting part of his face. In color they were dark brown, but each of them was ever so slightly out of line, so that when they focused on an object they looked like a pair of glass eyes. They focused now on Ben Grace, and presently shifted with a decidedly maniacal flicker. When Mr. Caspar spoke he shouted, his voice trembling with rage: "Listen, Ben, quit cracking dumb. You go to that meeting, and see you get there on time. If it's just voters, nuts. But if this guy's got friends, I got to know it. I got tipped today there's wise money back of him, that's figuring to knock me off. You know who they are, don't you?"

"I guess so."

"And you can see if they're there, can't you? If you want to you can find out what's going on, can't you?"

"O.K., Sol, but make it plain."

"And let me know."

"When?"

"Tomorrow."

"Where's the meeting?"

"Dewey High."

"All right, I'll be there."

"And take the bookies today."

"How do you get that way? Isn't it enough that I work tonight? Have I got to work all day too? This is supposed to be my day off."

Caspar's eyes fastened on Grace again, and he opened his mouth to say something, but at that moment Mrs. Caspar came in. She was a small, fat, bright-eyed Italian woman, leading a four-year-old boy, Franklin, by the hand. Grace jumped up when he saw her, and she nodded at him pleasantly, then began a report to Caspar, of the dentist's examination of Frankie's tooth. Ben, after giving Frankie a penny, started out. Caspar, however, hadn't forgotten him. "What do you say, Benny?"

"I say O.K."

In the big room, as Grace crossed it again, two men were sitting. One called himself Bugs Lenhardt, and sat reading a paper, near the door, where he could cover the slot with a minimum of effort. He was young, small, and vacant-eyed. The other, Lefty Gauss, had let Grace in, and now got up and walked out with him. He was of medium size and bandy-legged, with gray streaks in his hair and a frank, friendly air that suggested farms and other wholesome things. Actually he was a killer who had done considerable penal servitude, and the gray streaks in his hair came from operations in prisons, performed by doctors told off to get lead out of him, and not too particular how they did it. He and Grace stood silently in front of the elevators, then went down to the lobby, out to the street, and into a cocktail bar not far away with but a few glum words. It was only when they were settled in a dark corner that Ben began to talk and Gauss to listen.

Ben was full of grievances, some of them, such as his resentment that Caspar called him Benny, trivial, some of them, such as his dislike of gunfire, vital. This last he tried to place in an admirable light, as though it were a matter of citizenship, not fear. He insisted that he had never wanted his job in the first place, except temporarily when a serious injury ended his football career, and cited his refusal to wear a uniform as proof of his high-toned attitude. Yet a captious eavesdropper might have reflected that upright citizens do not as a rule become chauffeurs to notorious racketeers, whether they wear a uniform or not. Lefty listened sympathetically, shaking his beer to bring up the foam, nodding, and putting in understanding comment. Then presently he said, "Well, you got it tough, you sure have. But any time it gets too tough, just take a look at me."

"Anyway, he gives you a day off."

"Sometimes."

"And he don't stick you behind the wheel of a car that's armored behind but wide open in front, and every street named Goon Street as soon as *he* climbs aboard."

"Oh, no?"

"You too, hey?"

"Like today."

"Say, Lefty, what's going on today?"

"I got to split a heist, that's all."

"I didn't hear about it."

"They haven't got it yet. They're pulling it this afternoon—bank over in Castleton, right after closing time, the late depositor gag. *If* they pull it. If that depositor ever gets in, which isn't any more than a one to five bet."

"You'll know soon. It's three-thirty."

"Castleton's on mountain time."

"That's right. I forgot."

"You ever sat in on a divvy, Ben?"

"I don't know any yeggs."

"Four wild kids, anywhere from eighteen to twenty, scared so bad the slobber is running out of their mouths, couple of them coked to the ears, their suspenders stretched double from the gats they got in their pants. And Sol takes half, see? For protection, for giving them a place to lay up, he cuts off that much. O.K., he says part goes to the cops, but that don't help me any. There's the dough, all over the bed, in a room at the Globe Hotel. And there's the kids, kissing it and tasting it and smelling it. And there's me, that never seen one of them before, that hasn't got a pal in the bunch. I got to take half and get out. And maybe Sol crossed me. Maybe he *didn't* take care of the cops, and they come in on me, and it's ten years till the next beer. And for all that—now here's where it gets good—Solly, he slips me a hundred bucks."

"Why do we take it, what he dishes out?"

"Well, for one thing, bucking Sol is not healthy. And me, I *got* to take it. I'm not what I was. I don't get calls any more. To help on a job, I mean. I got to play along. You, of course you're different."

"In what way?"

"I figure you for a chiseler."

"What do you mean by that, Lefty?"

"That's all."

"Sounds like there might be more."

"Not unless you ask for it."

". . . O.K.—shoot."

"A chiseler, he's not crooked and he's not straight. He's just in between."

"Maybe he's just smart."

"I don't say he's not. I should say I don't. He takes it where he can get it, he's willing to live and let live, he don't want any trouble. If he can only hold it, what he's got, he'll die rich, and of a regular disease, with a doctor's certificate, 'stead of a coroner's. Still, he'll never be a big operator."

"Why not?"

"A big operator, he runs it, or he don't operate."

Lefty then gave a disquisition on the use of force: so long as Sol didn't mind trouble and Ben did, Sol would run it. It was diplomatically phrased, but Ben looked sulky, and Lefty added: "Listen, no hard feelings about it. Because maybe you're the one that *is* smart. You're putting it by all the time, or I *hope* you got that little savings account tucked away somewhere. You're young, and when Sol gets it you can always get a job."

"What do you mean, when Sol gets it?"

"Oh, he'll get it."

"You mean this Swede Jansen that's running for Mayor."

"He hasn't got a chance."

"He's got Sol worried."

"You mean Mayor Maddux has."

"I don't get it."

"Well, Sol's the main beneficiary of this, our present administration, isn't he? The boys had to figure some way to make him kick in. So Maddux told him who's back of the Swede."

"You mean Delany?"

"I mean our polo-playing, whiskey-drinking, white-tie-wearing, evil young man named Bill Delany, that gets by for a gentleman jockey but he's really a hoodlum bookie, and Sol has to cut him in whether he wants to or not, because he's got the Chicago connections. And for that reason Solly hates him so hard that all Maddux has to do is wink him in and he's there, even if he's not. Delany, he's got no more to do with the Swede than you have, but he could have. It could be the Swede that's going to knock Solly off. It could be anybody. For big enough dough, plenty guys don't mind trouble. One of them sees his disconnect button and leans on it, that's all."

"And then?"

"You're sitting pretty and I'm not."

"But *till* then, I'm his English setter."

"His—what did you say, Ben?"

"It's a dog, Lefty, and you ought to get next to them. They're white, with gray spots. They don't bark, they don't chase, and they don't fight. And when they point a bird, you can be sure it's a bird and not a skunk. In other words—me. Up at that meeting tonight."

"I didn't say so, Ben."

"A fine pair, we are."

"Well, when you come right down to it, nobody isn't so hot. Not really they're not. But if they're buddies, they can generally figure an angle. Me, I got one right away. Say what you will, we're prettier than Solly is."

"That's not saying much."

"It's practically not saying nothing at all. Still and all, I get a satisfaction out of it that I don't look like Solly looks."

"If it helps, then O.K."

"Two beers, Ben, and they're on you."

The bookmaking establishments to which Ben was assigned ran wide open in downtown office buildings, but with a two-hour time differential on account of Western tracks, there was nothing he could do about them until seven o'clock. Leaving Lefty, he went to the Lake City RKO to kill time. The theatre was named for the city, which had 220,000 inhabitants, a Chamber of Commerce, an airport, a war boom, and a Middle Western accent. The feature was a pleasant little item with Ginger Rogers in it, but the picture at which Ben laughed loudest and applauded most included Abbott and Costello. When he came out it was nearly six, and he walked around to his hotel. It was called the Lucas, and had $1-$1.50-$2 on the marquee. His room, for which he paid $8 a week, was on the second floor, but he didn't bother with the elevator. He bounded up the stairs with absentminded ease, first stopping at the desk to see if there had been any calls. His room was small, and had a single bed in it, a night table, a reading lamp, two straight chairs, a small armchair, and two water colors of nasturtiums. He paid not the least attention to it. He pitched his hat on the bed, stripped off his coat and shirt, and entered the shower. There, at the hand basin, he washed his face, ears, and neck, great muscles leaping out of his arms as he did so. Then he dried himself with a face towel, putting it back on the rack in its original creases. Then he combed his hair, tucking his forelock into place lovingly, with little brush strokes of the comb, and taking more time about it than the rite seemed to warrant.

Then he stepped into the room and had a look at his shirt. He frowned when he saw the collar, and dropped it into a laundry basket that stood in a closet. Then he selected another one from a shelf at the top of the closet. He put it on, chose a necktie to go with it, and when both had been patted into place, shoved the tail of his shirt into his trousers, and tightened his belt. His motions were precise, his person clean. And yet there was something of small dimension about everything he did. In this tiny room, with his boyish face, his neat little piles of rather well-bought possessions, it was hard to realize that he weighed at least 200 pounds.

The freshening completed, he went outside, walked down the street to the Savoy Grill, went inside and had dinner. He then walked to the Columbus, got a small satchel from the cashier, and visited the first of the bookmaking establishments. It was on the first floor of the Coolidge Building, past the elevators, and was full of men. They were in jovial mood, for two favorites had won, and they were there to cash tickets. With the big blackboard on one side of the room, the permanent column captions lettered thereon, and the businesslike atmosphere, the place suggested a stockbroker's office in Wall Street. Ben didn't attempt a thorough audit. He accepted an adding machine tote, crammed money and stub-books into his satchel, and went on to the next place. By a quarter to eight he had completed his rounds and left the satchel at the Columbus, first pasting a sticker over the clasp to seal it. Then he walked back to his hotel, passed through the lobby to an area-way behind, and entered a shed where cars were stored. His was a small coupe, maroon in color, with white tires and a high polish. He got in, checked the gas against an entry in a little red book that he took from his pocket, and drove off.

Municipal campaigns, as a rule, are held in the spring, with the election falling in May and the winner taking office July 1. So it happened that at John Dewey High School Auditorium it was a warmish night, with the crowd attending in spring dresses and straw hats. It was not, however, a very big crowd. Possibly five hundred people were there, half filling the auditorium; Lefty, apparently, had judged correctly the strength of the Jansen following. They were quiet, folksy people, and although Ben looked a little out of place among them, they smiled at him in friendly fashion as he came up the steps to the hall, and made way to let him in. He took a seat near the door, and began a systematic scrutiny of every face he could see. When the candidates arrived he joined the applause, and when the speaking began he frowned hard, concentrating on what was being said.

What was being said, alas, was a little slack. The offenses of Mr. Caspar, abetted by the Maddux machine, were the general topic, but nobody seemed to know quite what they were, and everybody left the indictment to somebody else. When Mr. Jansen spoke he was a grievous disappointment. He was a stocky, pink-faced, good-looking man with a little red moustache, but he had a thick accent, and did little but tell how Caspar had moved in on his milk truck drivers, "und den I make oop my mindt I mofe in on Caspar." The meeting was a flop until the chairman introduced a girl, quite as an afterthought, while people were crowding to the doors, and she started to talk.

She was a very good-looking girl, in spite of the school-teacherish way she spoke. She was perhaps twenty-five, with a trim little figure and solemn black eyes. She wore a dress of dark blue silk, which combined pleasantly with her wavy black hair, and she punctuated her remarks by tapping with a pencil on the table. Her point was that elections are not won with indignation, or talk, or registrations in the voters' books. They are won by ballots in the ballot box, and therefore she wanted everybody to stop at the table in the hallway, and fill out a slip with name, address, and phone number, and check what they would contribute on election day: time, car, or money, or all three. It was the first thing all night that had a resolute, professional sound to it, and once or twice it drew crackling applause. Ben got out his little red book, found the date, May 7, and wrote her name: June Lyons.

When Mr. Jansen came out of the school and entered his car, Ben was parked a few feet behind him, his lights out, his motor running. When Mr. Jansen started up, Ben started up, and seemed oddly expert at the job of following. On brightly lighted streets he cut his lights, and when he had to snap them on, fell back some distance, so the car ahead was not likely to notice him. Finally, when Mr. Jansen turned into the drive of a pretentious house in the swank Lakeside suburb, he parked nearby, and looked the place over, not missing the three Scandinavian birches growing in a cluster on the lawn. When another car drove up he watched Mr. Conley, the chairman; Mr. Bleeker, the candidate for

15

city attorney; Mrs. Bleeker and Miss Lyons get out and enter the house, then got out his little red book, and under May 7 again, copied down the number of the car. He sat a long time, waiting for other cars to appear. When the four visitors came out, he followed their car again, noting the addresses as Mr. and Mrs. Bleeker dropped their passengers off. It was around two o'clock when he tucked his little red book away and drove to Ike's Place, a small honky-tonk about four miles from town.

The place was fairly full and fairly noisy, with the crash of pinball shattering the beat of juke music. In the murk at one end of the bar a couple was dancing. Waiters in gray jackets with brass buttons hurried about, serving drinks; they were addressed by name, mostly, and treated the customers as old friends. When Ben came in he waved at Caspar, who was sitting at a table with Lefty, Bugs Lenhardt, another guard named Goose Groner, and two girls. Then he sat down at the bar, ordered a drink, and scanned a paper devoting its front page to the Castleton robbery, which had gone even worse than Lefty had expected. The four wild kids had got $22,000, but killed a cashier doing it.

Presently Groner was beside Ben, mumbling that Caspar wanted to see him. The girls moved over so Ben could sit down, but Caspar didn't invite him. Instead he demanded savagely to know where he had been. Ben, evidently deciding that an offense was the only defense against a stupid inquiry, stuck out his chin and said: "Me? I been working. I been carrying out orders, some kind of hop dreams that were thought up by a jerk named Solly Caspar—no relation, I hope. I been tailing a Swede all over town, and copying down the car numbers of his friends, and making a sap out of

16

myself—wasn't that a way to spend a spring night! And for what? Because they been taking this lug, this fathead named Caspar, for a ride the whole town is laughing at."

"Ride? What ride?"

"Come on, get wise to yourself. The ride Maddux is taking you for. Filling you up with that hooey about Delany—"

"Oh, so you think it's hooey?"

"Listen, I've seen this Swede's friends, and they wouldn't know Delany if they met him on the street. It's a gyp and you fell for it, that's all."

Ben got this off with quite a show of truculence, and it left Caspar blinking, and would probably have settled the argument if he hadn't slightly overplayed it. He took up the previous question, which was where he had been all night, reminding Caspar it had been clearly stipulated that he was not to report until tomorrow; and when Caspar weakly tapped his watch and said it *was* tomorrow, he said that as far as he was concerned it was not tomorrow until the sun came up. At this one of the girls, who had been eyeing Ben's curls with more than casual interest, let out an appreciative laugh. Caspar's eyes flickered. Lefty jumped up and began telling him a story, a meaningless thing about a couple of Irishmen that went into a hotel. Groner began whispering to him, patting his back and leaning close to his ear. The girl, frightened, poked him with her finger, and said hey, quit scaring her to death.

This went on for five minutes, and the place froze like a cinematic stop-camera shot. Ike, the proprietor, caught the eye of the bartender, who stood with a shaker in his hand, checking the position of the waiters. These came to a stop in the aisles, and stood staring at Caspar.

He began to pant, and when Groner touched his arm, shook it as though something had stung him. Then, his seizure passing, he screamed: "O.K., you took the car number! Why don't you pass it over? What you waiting for?"

Ben, who had turned green, stared at him. He stared a long time, his eyes becoming small, cold, and hard. Then he took out his little red book, copied a number on the back of a beer mat, and rolled it to Caspar. Before returning the book to his pocket he creased the page with his thumbnail. But this page was not captioned May 7.

It was captioned April 29.

2

Next afternoon, when Ben reported to work, Sol was in high good humor. He indulged in a little heavy-handed kidding, played a new swing record, and in other small ways tried to atone for his behavior of the previous night. Presently he said: "And was *you* fooled!"

"Yeah? How?"

"Them guys. That you seen with Jansen."

"Oh? You know who they were?"

"I had that license checked. The one you give me last night. I sent a special wire to Chicago, and I just now got a reply. You know who that car belonged to?"

"I got no idea."

"Frankie Horizon."

"Well, say—and he looked like another Swede."

"How many times I got to tell you, you can't go by

their looks. Frankie Horizon—and him and Delany are just like that."

Sol held up two fingers to indicate a close degree of intimacy, as Ben stared incredulously. Compassionately, then, Sol shook his head. "I don't know what I'm going to do about you, Ben."

"How you mean, Sol?"

"Them Illinois plates. Didn't they mean nothing to you?"

"Well—plenty people live in Illinois."

"Wise money has generally got Illinois plates."

"I'll try to remember."

"It's O.K.—if you could remember something you wouldn't be driving a car, for me or anybody. And, you found out what I wanted, so take tomorrow off."

"Well, gee, thanks, Sol."

"That's a promise. Go on, make a date."

In the big room, however, Lefty seemed even more dejected, if that were possible, than he had been yesterday. He sat tipping one key of the piano, and when Ben presently asked him to cut it out, he announced: "He's going to die."

"*Who's* going to die?"

"That kid. That got it at Castleton yesterday."

"How you know he's going to die?"

"That doc, the look on his face."

"Where's the kid shot?"

"In the hip."

"Did the doc get the bullet out?"

"It came in and went out. The guard, before they got out of the bank, had time to grab his rifle, and it was with that that the kid got it, just a little hole that went right through. He's not in any pain. He thinks he's going to be moving soon. But the other three, they can see him behind, where he's turning black. They're getting jittery. They're getting worse than I am."

The shrug that Ben gave was perhaps more indifferent than one would expect, on a warm afternoon, at a piece of news of at least average quality, with nothing else to talk about. It was matched by the yawn he gave next morning, when Lefty arrived at the Lucas before he was up, and sat on the edge of the bed, and furnished a few more details. "His temperature's up, Ben. He's beginning to rave. And the other three, I don't know what they'll pull. They're liable to conk him to make him shut up or something. They're not old-timers. They're just kids. They don't know what to do when a guy gets it. And the hotel, they're turning on the heat."

"Can't you get him out of there?"

"Where to?"

It was at this point that Ben yawned, and Lefty went on: "What am I going to do, Ben? *He's going to die, and what am I going to do with him?* I can't serve no more time. I can't take it. I was already stir crazy, a little bit . . ."

"Dogged if I know what to tell you."

When Lefty went, Ben got up, held the door on a crack, and peeped down the hall, to make sure he was really gone. Then, on his outside phone, he dialed a number and asked for Miss Lyons—Miss June Lyons.

A girl slowing down as a man held up a newspaper, the man climbing into the car she was driving, the two of them going on at the change of the light—it looked casual enough, yet it had been planned by Ben, and carried out by her, in such fashion as to make it impossible that they should be followed. She was driving Mr. Jansen's big green sedan, and for a few moments they studied each other. Then he laughed. "Hey, cut that out. Smile. Relax."

"You mean the frown?"

"It's just terrible."

"That's what my mother always says."

"You must have had it a long time if she's always saying."

"It comes from taking things seriously."

"What things?"

"Oh—this and that."

"Not Jansen?"

"Well, why not Jansen?"

"I wouldn't think he'd appeal to you. Fact of the matter, ever since I heard you make that speech the other night, I've been wondering why you're hooked up with him. You look serious enough, but you don't look dumb enough."

"Well, Jansen isn't really what I meant."

"And what did you mean?"

"Something personal."

"Romance?"

"I'd hardly take *that* seriously."

She was smiling now, and her face lighted up quite pleasantly, though there was still something solemn about it, as though back of any light idea that entered her mind there would always be some sobering consideration. He smiled a little too, and said: "If it's not love it's got to be money."

"It might be a little of both, but not the way you mean. Since my frown seems to interest you, and my connection with Mr. Jansen seems to interest you, they both have to do with my family, and it's a long story, and not at all exciting, and I'd rather not talk about it, if you don't mind."

"Your family live here?"

"Do *you* live here?"

"Looks like we got a little dead-end there."

"If, as you said over the phone, I'm not to ask questions about who you are, or anything about you, then don't ask questions about me, or my family, or where they live. What is this business you and I have, anyway? After that call, the very least I expected was a blue chin and a broken nose."

"You disappointed?"

"A little."

"I called about Jansen."

"Oh, the dumb candidate."

"He's dumb, but outside of Maddux he's the only candidate we've got, anyway, that's got his papers filed. So I've been looking him over. So I've been thinking it might be a good idea if he was elected, or perhaps I should say, if Maddux was defeated."

"And?"

"I'm kicking in with a little dirt."

"I'd rather have money, but—"

"You'll settle for dirt. You know the Castleton robbery?"

"The bank?"

"That's it. Suppose friend Jansen found out where that mob was hiding. Suppose he found out they were here, in Lake City, under protection of Caspar and the police department. Suppose he found out the exact hotel. Could he use it?"

Not waiting for a reply, Ben took out an envelope, tore off the back, and wrote down four names. "There they are. They're at the Globe Hotel, Room 38, a double room with two extra cots moved in. That last guy, Rossi, the one I checked, is shot. He's going to die, so if Jansen is going to use this he better do it quick. When he does die, the other three will certainly skip."

Ben was obviously surprised at the hostile stare she turned on him. With an ironical laugh she said: "You must have gone to college, didn't you? To think up one like that?"

"Like what, for instance?"

"It's criminal libel, that's all—if Mr. Jansen mentions the name of the hotel, and not worth a plugged dime if he doesn't. And coming now, just a week before election, it's a trick, I would say, to send Mr. Jansen to the polls under indictment, and perhaps even under arrest. To say nothing of what could be done to his business and property in the civil action, later."

"You're a smart girl, aren't you?"

"Oh, I went to college too. And law school."

"You're about as dumb a girl as any candidate ever had back of him. Here I offer you dirt, and the first thing you tell me is that you'd rather have money. Well June, there comes a time when money's not enough. You've got to have dirt—not nice clean dirt, like calling names and all this stuff Jansen has been handing out. Dirty dirt. Dirt that stinks so bad something has to be done about it. And here I offer you some, with more to come, much as you want, enough to break Caspar and all the rest of them, and all you see in it is criminal libel. I guess you belong with Jansen, come to think of it. And now suppose we go back. Sitting this close to you makes me feel a little sick to my stomach."

She drove a little further, her face getting redder

and redder. Then she turned around, and when they came to a car track he motioned her to stop. When he got out he didn't say goodbye.

After dinner, he walked slowly down Hobart Street, looking at movie notices, but none of them seemed to suit him. He went back to his hotel, entered his room, and lay down, first removing his coat and hanging it in the closet. In a moment or two his fingers found the radio, which was tucked on the second deck of the night table, and turned it on. For the better part of an hour he lay there, the light off, listening to dinner music from the Columbus. Then the Jansen meeting came in, and he scowled, starting to turn it off. Then he changed his mind and lay there listening, his face a sombre shadow in the half dark, while the same old speeches came in that he had listened to at the high school. When June was introduced he made a second motion to cut the radio off, and again changed his mind. Then suddenly he sat up in bed, and snapped on the light, and listened with rapt attention.

She was talking about the hook-up, the alliance between crime, the Mayor, and the police, and even the crowd sensed that she was leading up to something. Then with breath-taking suddenness it came: "You think there's no hook-up, do you? You think that's something *we* invented, to get Mr. Jansen elected? Then why are those four bandits, the ones that robbed the Security Bank at Castleton day before yesterday, the ones that took $22,000 from that bank and murdered Guy Horner, the cashier—why are they hiding in Lake City? Why are Buck Harper, Mort Dubois, Boogie-Woogie Lipsky, and Arch Rossi in the Globe Hotel right now, with nothing being done about them? You think Chief Dietz doesn't know about them? He does, because he told me so. I called him at four o'clock this afternoon, and told him I was the operator at the Globe Hotel, and asked him if there were any further instructions on the party of four in Room 38. He said: 'Not till Arch Rossi gets so he can travel, anyhow. But I'm not really handling it. You better talk to Solly Caspar.' "

The snarl from the crowd had an echo of the wolf pack in it, but June shouted over it: "Will somebody stop that officer? The one that's trying to get out, to telephone?"

Evidently the officer stopped, for there was a big laugh, and June said: "There's no use warning those boys, officer. You see, after I talked to Chief Dietz I called Castleton, and the Castleton detectives are at the hotel right now, and I think they'll move a little too fast for you to stop them—a little official kidnapping, so to speak. It's the only way, apparently, to bring murderers to trial under the conditions we have in Lake City."

An exultant light in his eye, Ben snapped off the radio. Then, moving with catlike silence, he went to the door, jerked it open. The hall was empty. Then he put on his coat, picked up his hat, and went out to the Tracy picture at the Rialto.

When he came in, Mr. Nerny, the elderly night clerk, was signaling with one hand. "Call for you, Mr. Grace. Party was just about to hang up when I told them I was quite sure I recognized your step. Take it down here if you like."

Into the house phone, Ben said: "Hello?"

"Mr. Grace?"

"Speaking."

"This is your friend that takes things seriously."

"*Who?*"

"The one you went riding with, today."

"Oh yes. I'll call you later. Goodbye."

Hanging up, he shot a glance at Mr. Nerny, but Mr. Nerny had put aside his earphones, and apparently had heard nothing. Upstairs, he paced about, and started to take off his clothes. But the knowledge that this girl knew who he was evidently threw him badly off step, and presently he clapped on his hat and went out.

"What was the idea, calling me?"

"Well, it was pretty successful, what I did. What you did. What—we did. I thought, after the way I acted today, the least I could do was call you and thank you."

"Over that hotel phone?"

"Oh, I was going to be careful."

"On a night like this, when we set off five tons of dynamite in this town, you were going to let a night clerk hear you being careful?"

"Is it as melodramatic as that?"

"Yeah."

He turned away from her, and became aware of the apartment she lived in. It was a bare little place, almost shabby, on the second floor of a small apartment house. To one side was a dining alcove, and a double door looked as though a bed might lurk behind it. He had not got up here without an argument through the door phone, for it was at least one o'clock in the morning, and when she finally let him up, she made him wait five minutes while she put on these lounging pajamas that she now wore. They were dark red, and certainly becoming, but he paid no attention to them. As she continued to smile, he seized her roughly by the arm and asked: "What's so funny about this melodrama thing? . . . O.K., they shoot off blanks, and I guess that's funny. But Caspar, he don't shoot off blanks. When he shoots, he throws lead. Is that funny? Go on, let's see you laugh."

She tried to pull her arm away, but he gave it another shake. "And how'd you find out who I am, by the way?"

"I don't see that that matters."

"Oh yes. It matters."

She turned to a table, opened a drawer, and took out a piece of paper. "When you tear up envelopes to write on, you might burn the part that has your name and address on it, or put it back in your pocket, or something. You were in such a hurry to jump out of the car today that you left this on the seat."

"And who did you show it to?"

"Nobody."

"And who did you tell about it?"

"Nobody."

"Come on! How about Jansen?"

"About you, I've told nothing, and I can prove it."

"O.K., prove."

"Were you there? At the meeting?"

"I heard it."

"You noticed I made that announcement myself?"

"Saving Jansen from criminal libel?"

"After I called Dietz and made sure that what you told me was true, I didn't have to worry about libel. No, I was thinking about myself. I was making sure that I, and nobody else, got the credit. I wanted to be certain that Mr. Jansen, if he gets elected, will have to do a lot more about me in the shape of a job than he would have to do if I was just a girl that handled secretaries, and had slips filled out. In that case I wouldn't be telling anybody the source of my information, would I? You see, I'm hoping for *more* tips."

He sat down and studied her intently. Relaxing, she sat down, not far away, on the same hard little sofa. Suddenly he asked: "Outside of my name, do you know who I am?"

"No."

"I'm Sol Caspar's driver."

"Then—you're Sol Caspar's driver."

"And that's O.K. with you?"

"It certainly gilt-edges your tips."

"And it don't bother you that I drive for him six days a week and then on my day off I call you up and give you tips?"

"I'm willing to believe you have your reasons."

"I got plenty of reasons."

"Then—I'm glad to know that."

"I'd rather fight him clean, right out in the open, the way you fight him. I'd be perfectly willing to quit my job, and tell him straight out what I'm up to, than knife him in the back this way. But if I could quit my job I wouldn't be fighting him at all. I'm not looking for trouble. He even laughs at me because I don't *like* trouble. But he won't let me quit. If I quit, it's curtains for me, and that's why I'm here with you. He asked for it. I didn't."

"I'm *very* glad to know that."

"O.K. Now who are you?"

"Nobody."

"Listen, I've got to know."

"I was born in Ohio, and raised there, just across the river from Kentucky. I went to school there, and high school, and college, and law school. Then I heard of a job in Lake City, and applied for it, and got it, and came here."

"What kind of a job?"

"With a law firm, Wiener, Jacks, and Myers. They pay me a salary, about as good a salary as young lawyers get, more than you might think from this." She waved her hand at the apartment. "I only keep part of my salary for myself. And—I've got to have still more money. I simply *must* have it."

"Why you more than somebody else?"

"I told you it's a long story."

"More family history?"

"It's been going on a long time, and I'd rather not go into it. Anyway, Jansen came along. I'd done a little work for him, settling claims. And he was thinking about running for Mayor. And I was thinking about a job, one of those heavenly city hall jobs where you come down once a week to sign papers, and hold your regular job just the same. And—I guess I egged him on."

"For the dough?"

"Not entirely. I think he's a fine man, fit to be Mayor, a hundred times better than Maddux. Just the same—"

"The dough is the main thing?"

"Now I feel like a heel."

"No need to feel that way. Listen, if it was just idealism, I might give you tips, but I'd be plenty worried. I don't believe in that stuff, and I don't believe in people that do believe in it. Now I know it's the old do-re-mi, that's different. O.K., June. We can do business."

"I'm afraid it *is* idealism, just the same."

"You said it was dough."

"Yes, but not to have it, or spend it, or whatever people do with it. Money, just as money, doesn't mean much to me. But as a means to an end, as something that will permit me to deal with—a certain situation—"

"Back home?"

"It might be. Well, money for that purpose is important to me. Then it will mean something to me."

"Are you out to get it or not?"

"Indeed I am."

"That's all I want to know."

She got the solemn frown on her face again, as though she wanted to make clear that it was no ordinary greed that prompted her present activities, but he ran his finger up the crease between her brows. She laughed. "I want to be an idealist."

"O.K., so I'm a chiseler."

"Oh, say *crook*."

"A chiseler, he's not a crook."

"He certainly isn't honest."

"He's just in between."

Two days before, when Lefty had said it, Ben had obviously been annoyed. Now, just as obviously, he was beginning to be proud of it. She laughed. "Anyway, we're both walloping Caspar."

"I hope we are."

"But look *how* we're walloping him."

She got a paper from the alcove, and came back with it. It was a midnight edition, and all over the front page was the story of how the Castleton detectives had raided the Globe Hotel and grabbed three of the bandits without bothering to get in touch with the Lake City police. Ben seemed surprised that only three bandits were

31

bagged, and she explained: "The other one, the one that was shot, had been taken away before the Castleton police got there."

"Alive?"

"We think so."

He was already reading the news story, but she pointed to the editorial, also on Page 1, and he read it with her, their heads nearly touching. It attacked Castleton savagely, but went on to say that the charges made by Miss June Lyons, a speaker at the Jansen meeting, were too serious to be ignored. An investigation of the Lake City police department should be made, and if Mayor Maddux wouldn't act, the Governor ought to. "It's the first time, Mr. Grace—"

"Call me Ben."

"It's the first time, Ben, that either of the big papers has taken us seriously. The little *News-Times* does what it can, but this is the *Post!* If I just had a little *more* dirt . . ."

"You *are* waking up, aren't you?"

"I'll say I am."

She was breathless, tense, eager. For a second their eyes met, and it seemed queer that he suddenly got up, instead of taking her in his arms, which he certainly could have done. He stood uncertainly for a moment, then picked up his hat. "One thing."

"Yes?"

"Tell Jansen to put a private guard on here. Outside, at least two men, day and night. I'd do it, but they'd know me. Ring him soon as I go, and have him attend to it tonight. *Tonight,* see? That's necessary, after what you did, and a Lake City police guard is the same as no guard at all. You hear me?"

"All right, I'll call him."
"I'll ring you tomorrow. With maybe more dirt."
"I'll see you soon, Ben."
"That's right. Soon."

3

Lefty sat down with Ben next morning as he was having breakfast in the Savoy Grill. A toothpick indicated he himself had already eaten, and he began without preliminaries: "Well, it's war."

"Blitz or sitz?"

"Blitz, I'd say. Sol and Delany."

"What's Delany done?"

"You heard what happened last night?"

"I'm reading about it."

"If it was just tipping that girl, O.K. It wasn't friendly, but after them sharpshooters you seen with Jansen, Solly knew what to expect. But about an hour before the Castleton bulls got there, a Delany guy shows up, a guy that takes care of his horses, over at the Jardine stables. And he takes Arch Rossi out. He takes him out of the Globe and over to the Columbus. Sol, he don't like that. If the kid has to die, he could die just as good in Castleton, couldn't he? In a hospital, with good doctors taking care of him? Dumping him in the Columbus, right in Solly's own hotel, Solly takes that personal."

"So?"

"He's taking steps."

"Where *is* Delany?"

"He's in Chicago, but he'll come back."

"If coaxed?"

"On proper inducements, he'll come."

"Where's Rossi?"

"I don't exactly know."

Lefty stared vacantly at the hat stand across the room, laid the toothpick in an ashtray. "So it'll be an O.K. war, if that's getting us anywheres, and Solly, of course, he'll be nice and happy. Just the same, it's not Delany."

"Then who is it?"

"I figured it might be you."

As Lefty turned his cold, vacant stare full on Ben's face, Ben lit a cigarette. He let the match burn for a moment, and from the interested way he looked at it, one might wonder if he was testing, to know if his hand was trembling. When there was not the slightest flicker, he blew the match out, and asked languidly: "You tell Sol that?"

"Yeah."

"What'd he say?"

"He didn't believe it."

"But you, my old pal, you believe it, don't you?"

"Listen, Ben, I'm your pal, but this ain't the candy business. In this racket you can't take chances, and if you're crossing us, the pal stuff is out. Couple of things look pretty funny to me. If there was a couple of sharp-shooters with Jansen the other night, both pals of Delany, why didn't you know it? Seemed a little off the groove that Solly had to find that out. And why would Delany start something? He's sitting pretty. On the bookies he gets his cut and it's not hay. He's got a nice daily double and he don't even have to stay here and watch it. Why would he bust it up?"

"And that leaves me, hey?"

"It could."

"Nuts."

"Oh, yeah?"

"Lefty, you're playing it safe, you got to do that. You got to feed me a lead and watch my face, just like I'd do for you, just like all pals got to do to each other in this swell business we're in. But you don't really think it's me. If you did you'd just rub me out and that would be that. Even if you halfway thought it was me, you'd have fed me a phoney just now, on where you're keeping Arch Rossi, and then if I ran to her with it you'd have me. When you didn't do at least that much I know you're not really bearing down."

"O.K., Ben. But it's *somebody,* and I'm worried."

"I'm a little worried myself."

"Then we're both worried."

"Pals?"

"Two beers, and they're on you."

Around nine, when Ben went back to his hotel, the day clerk said a lady had called, twice. He went to his room and dialed June, getting no answer. In five minutes his house phone rang, and when June spoke he gave her the number of his outside phone. Only when she had called him on this did he let her go ahead. "Something's happened, Ben."

"O.K., give."

"It's the boy that took Rossi out of the Globe."

"And what about him?"

"He showed up at Jansen's about an hour ago, and Jansen called me. I wouldn't let them come to my apartment, but I met them outside, and—I don't know what to do with him. He's been wandering around all night, and he's afraid to go home, for fear he'll be killed, and he can't go to the police, because they're hand-in-glove with Caspar, and—"

"Where are you now?"

"In a drug store, and he and Jansen are outside—"

"Don't say who I am, but get him to the phone."

In a few moments the boy was on the line, and Ben talked with the stern tone of a Governor, or at the very least of a prosecuting attorney. "What's your name?"

"Herndon, sir. Bob Herndon."

"And what's this about Arch Rossi?"

"Nothing, sir. I swear I never knew he was mixed up in the Castleton robbery. Me and Arch, we went to school together, and we was buddies. Then I didn't see him for a while, and then yesterday he called me, over at the Jardine stables, where I work for Mr. Delany."

"Bill Delany or Dick Delany?"

"Mr. Bill, sir."

"What do you do for him?"

"I take care of his horses, sir, all six of his polo ponies and his two thoroughbred mares. Of course I got to get help exercising them, but—"

"O.K., so Arch Rossi called you?"

"Yes sir, he said he'd been hurt in a car accident, and he was in Room 38 at the Globe, and would I call a taxi and come over and get him out of there. I thought it was kind of funny, and I couldn't do anything till six o'clock, when I was off, but then he called again, and when he said he had plenty of dough I called a cab and went over there. There were three other guys there, and they cussed Arch out and told him to get out and stay out. So I figured if it was a car accident, maybe the car was stolen. Then from the way Arch began talking in the cab I knew he was shot. Then when we got to the Columbus and I was helping him in through the service entrance I heard somebody say: 'Holy smoke, here comes one of those Castleton rats,' and I looked around and it was a guy that runs the Columbus for Caspar by the name of Henry Hardcastle."

"You know Henry Hardcastle?"

"I seen him at the track plenty of times."

"He know you?"

"I'll say he does."

"Herndon, what are you lying to me for?"

"Mister, I'm not lying."

"If Rossi was shot, why would he be leaving the Globe, unless he got orders? And if it was orders, why don't you say so? And if you're working for Caspar, what's the big idea, going to Mr. Jansen and handing him a lot of chatter about being afraid to go home?"

"I don't work for Caspar."

"Then it don't make sense."

"It makes sense if you heard what Arch was saying in the cab. He was shot, see? And he was laying up with three guys that he was afraid would knock him off just to get rid of him. And nothing was being done about him except a bum doctor would come in every day and tell him he was getting along swell. But from the way the other three were whispering he knew he wasn't

38

getting along swell, and he figured his only chance was to get to Caspar, so—"

"O.K. Now it makes sense. Go on."

"That's all, except when I tumbled to what it was all about I beat it, and when I got home my sister was yelling out the window at me to go away, that they were after me, and I had to beat it again. And I been beating it ever since, and I don't know who you are, Mister, but if you got some place I can go, then—"

"Is the lady still there?"

"Yes, sir."

"Put her on and get back to the car."

When June answered again, Ben spoke rapidly and decisively. "O.K., the first thing you do, you shoot this bird over to Castleton. Have Jansen take him over in person, and start at once. As soon as they're gone, get over to Jansen headquarters, call the Castleton police and let them know what's coming. Then sit tight. Be at Jansen headquarters all day, just in case."

"Have Jansen take him in person?"

"That's it. We're playing in luck, terrific luck. This Herndon, he's just a lug that curries horses. But he curries them for Delany, and that's all we need. Solly fell for it last night, and he'll keep on falling for it if we just let him. We got him chasing his own tail and he don't know it."

"I'm terribly excited."

"Get going."

"I'm off."

Hanging up, Ben sat down on the unmade bed, his watch in his hand. At the end of fifteen minutes he dialed the *Pioneer*. "City desk, please . . . Hello, you want a tip on that bandit, Arch Rossi?"

"What do you think?"

"O.K., I can't tell you where he is, but I can tell you where his pal is, and if you hop on it, maybe you can get some dope from him."

"I'll bite, where is he?"

"Castleton."

"Why?"

"Caspar was after him, for dropping Rossi at the Columbus. He was afraid to go home, and he went to Jansen. So Jansen's taking him to the Castleton cops, for protection and maybe some evidence. They started ten or fifteen minutes ago, in Jansen's car."

"Who are you?"

"Little Jack Horner."

"O.K., Jack. Thanks."

When the first editions came out, it developed that the newspaper had done what Ben no doubt expected. It had chartered a special plane, and had reporters and photographers waiting when Jansen walked into Castleton police headquarters with Herndon. In the big room, Ben and Lefty read silently, studied the pictures of Jansen, of Herndon, even of Rossi, in a blown-up snapshot that somebody had dug up. The buzzer kept sounding, and Lefty kept jumping up to admit various personages: Jack Brady, secretary to the Mayor; Inspector Cantrell, of the Police Department; James Joseph Bresnahan, ace reporter for the *Pioneer;* photographers, bellboys, telegraph messengers. The Bresnahan interview broke for the financial edition, and Lefty began to curse when he read it. It was mainly Bresnahan, in an F. Scott Fitzgerald picture of Caspar, as though he were a great Gatsby of some credit to the town. But it was quite a little Caspar, too, in an interview that gave no names, but intimated all too plainly that if the citizenry wanted to know more about Rossi, or of the various scandals that had recently rocked the town, it might ask a certain society racketeer who knew much more than many might think.

In the five-star final, there was a picture of Dick Delany, standing beside his car, about to depart for Chicago, where, it was explained, he would interview his brother, as special correspondent for the paper, and find out what truth there might be in the Caspar charges, or in the various rumors that were flying around. When he saw this, Ben managed a fair imitation of a snicker. "Say, that's a laugh—they're hiring Dick Delany to drive over to Chicago and interview Bill on what Solly's saying about him."

"I see they are."

"I guess Sol's not in any real danger."

"How you figure that out?"

"If they really mean it, why don't they put a real reporter on it? What's the idea of sending Dick Delany, that stumblebum that don't hardly know right from left? To me, that looks quite a lot like a coat of whitewash."

"To me it looks different."

"Yeah? How so?"

"What you say, that would be O.K. if Solly had it doped right. If Delany *was* back of this stuff that's being sprung by the Jansen people, and especially that girl, then sending Dick over would be about the dumbest play they could think up, because it would just be helping him cover up. But if Solly's got it wrong, and Delany's a little sore, and wants to shoot off his mouth, then Dick would just be the perfect guy for him to talk to, wouldn't it? To *me*—of course nobody pays any attention to what I say around here any more, and it's just one mug's opinion—but to me it looks like they straightened Solly up for the old one-two and no bell to save him. First they send Bresnahan over here and get him to shoot off his face, and you'll notice Dick's got that paper in his hand even while he's having his picture taken. If Bill needed anything more to open him up, that would do it."

Carefully, Lefty read the *Pioneer*'s write-up of Mr. Bill Delany; of his start as a hostler in the Jardine stables; of his rise to riding instructor, to exhibitor of mounts at local horse shows; of his acquisition of various runners, particularly Golden Bough, a winner of purses some years before; of his reputed share in several tracks; of the rumors that connected him with organized gambling. As to this, however, the *Pioneer* was quite sketchy, and even jocular, as though nobody really believed the rumors, except perhaps Mr. Caspar. Then it went on to relate the strange relationship between Bill and his brother Dick; how the older brother self-effacingly kept behind the scenes, letting the younger brother do the family manners; how this last "tall, handsome, hard-riding man-about-town" had quite captured Lake City's imagination; how he entered horses at the leading tracks, played in local polo games, belonged to several clubs, including the Lakeside Country Club, and had been reported engaged to several of the younger members of the social set. As to his brains, or lack of them, the paper had nothing to say, unless something was to be inferred from the paragraph: "Yet it is an open secret that the man behind the silks is not Dick, but Bill. Not that Dick is merely a 'front' for his quite active brother. On the contrary, he leads a pretty full life on his own account. And yet it is Bill, not Dick, who captains the ship, buys the gee-gees, decides where they are to be entered."

Lefty shook his head. "You got it wrong, Ben. If the *Pioneer* was all, they mean it plenty."

"What do you mean, if the *Pioneer* was all?"

"I told you, we're taking steps."

"Oh, that's right, I forgot."

"Maybe one too many."

Pioneer Park, the local baseball grounds, was in striking contrast with John Dewey High School, just a few nights before. There the crowd had been small, quiet, and dispirited. Here, as a result of the sensational revelations of the last day or two, thousands of people were gathered, in a tense, excited mood. They overflowed from the space back of home plate, where seats had been placed, into the stand itself. On the speakers' stand that had been erected over the plate floodlights glared down, and as the loudspeakers carried every word that was said to the far corners of the grounds, loud cheers went up, with occasional calls for June, the mystery girl of the campaign.

Mr. Caspar arrived around eight, riding between Goose and Bugs on the back seat of the big armored sedan, with Ben at the wheel and Lefty beside Ben. Just what he was doing there, to judge from what was being said, was a puzzle to everybody in the car, and an unwelcome one, at that. His own explanation was: "It's time I had a look at that dame"; and this, coupled with his compulsion to show his power wherever he could, seemed to be about the only reason. His power was evident at once. The car no sooner arrived than a sergeant waved it past the turnstiles, where lesser folks entered to the vehicle gate, which he ordered open. There a motorcycle patrolman picked it up, and led it past the rear of the grandstand to a point where the bleachers ended, and from there to a dark spot just back of the coaching lines. Several other cars were parked on the infield. Bugs jumped out, to look them over, and keep an eye on things behind. But Sol paid no attention, and made remarks at the expense of the speakers. One of them, soliciting money, said that three $1,000 contributions had been received in the last twenty-four hours, and to this Sol said: "Three thousand bucks! Wha ya know about that! Gee, they don't look out they're gonna have enough to pay for a coupla funerals."

"Hey, Solly, cut it out."

"Three funerals, grand apiece."

"I said cut it out."

Lefty, as Sol made no effort to muffle his jibes, was growing increasingly nervous. Presently, after the crowd had been lashed to a frenzy by several speakers, by excerpts from the day's newspapers, by a brief speech from Jansen, June was introduced, and stepped into view, under the lights. The ensuing demonstration lasted five minutes, and Sol paid his respects to her clothes, her figure, and her general appearance, laughing loudly at his not very delicate sallies. But when she began to speak he fell as silent as he might have if he had been hit with an axe. "Mr. Chairman, honorable candidates, fellow citizens, Mr. Caspar."

"There it goes."

Lefty, perhaps with reason, obviously blamed the jocosity of the last half hour for June's knowledge of their presence. Sol froze into a small, compact ball as she lifted the mike, turned it around, and faced him, her back to the major portion of the crowd. "I'm glad you've seen fit to honor us with your presence, Mr. Caspar, be-

44

cause I've information that will interest you as a hotel owner. You were correctly quoted, I assume, in Mr. Bresnahan's article in today's *Pioneer,* in which you said that nobody by the name of Rossi, so far as you know, is staying at the Columbus Hotel. I must regretfully report that you don't know everything that goes on at the Columbus. Mr. Arch Rossi is at the Columbus, this very minute. He must be there, because I myself talked with him, less than an hour ago. Of course I had some difficulty getting him on the line. I had to put the call through Castleton police headquarters, and make it appear as though Bob Herndon was trying to talk to his old pal, and tell him things that might be of interest—"

There was a warning shout from Bugs, watching behind. Then lights flashed all around the car. The photographers, who were out in force, had probably started together, as soon as June started to speak. At any rate they had the car surrounded, and were snapping furiously to get pictures. Caspar began pounding Ben on the back, ordering him to get out of there. Ben spun his motor, fast. The outfield floodlights came on, as the crowd gave a roaring laugh. Ben, his head twisted backwards, caught the horn with his elbow, and it brayed grotesquely. The crowd gave a cheer. It seemed minutes before they cleared the bleachers, and were whirling away.

"Boy, you ought to hear them. I don't know where that dame came from, but she's going to cost Maddux the election if something's not done. Sol, he better look out."

Bugs, left in the ball park by the circumstance that cars have no running boards any more for lookout men to jump on, climbed in beside Ben, who was parked in the areaway back of the Columbus. "She's stirring 'em up, hey?"

"It's just murder. After you left she cut it loose and what she don't know about this outfit ain't hardly worth knowing. Where's Sol?"

"Inside."

"Goose and Lefty with him?"

"Yeah, but he said wait. We're going somewhere."

"Sure, with Arch Rossi."

"Oh, yeah?"

"He's got to get rid of the kid, hasn't he? Boy, after what that dame told them out there tonight he can't have him here any more. Not in the Columbus, he can't."

"What do you mean, get rid of him?"

"Ben, if I knew I wouldn't say."

When Sol came out of the hotel, however, he was alone. He climbed in the car and sat smoking, as though waiting for something. Presently, from the street, came the sound of police sirens. From where they were sitting they could see several cars pull up in front on the street, and spew officers all over the sidewalk. These disappeared, and Sol tiptoed to the rear of the hotel to listen. Bugs nodded at Ben, whispered that Solly was on the job, all right, and probably had the thing under control. This raid meant that Rossi was already out of the hotel, and the cops would find nothing. Even before the police cars had pulled away Sol was back in the car, and told Ben to drive to Memorial Boulevard. Bugs moved to the back seat with him, and they started out.

They drove out Memorial into a black, bleary waste of suburbs not yet become open country. Then Sol said to stop. When they were at a standstill, he told Ben to wink his lights. At once they got a wink in return from a side road, some distance ahead. Then Sol told Ben to keep the lights dark, and run to the other car. Cautiously Ben rolled ahead in the dark, but stopped at the sound of running footsteps. The footsteps drew nearer, while all three of them sat silent. Then Lefty was beside the car, his voice lifted in a quavering wail: "They've plugged him, Solly, they've plugged him—*they've plugged him!*"

Sol got out, followed by Bugs, and with apparent concern inquired: "Where they at?" But Lefty, as he turned to point, hit the ground in a sprawl, and the breath left his body in a grunting sob. Sol jumped on him, jammed his knee in his stomach, and slapped him eight, ten, or a dozen times. Then he told Bugs to give him a gun, and when Bugs drew one from an armpit holster, jammed it at Lefty's mouth. Lefty clenched his teeth, striking at Sol with his fists. Bugs seized his arms and held them against the ground. Sol pulled his cheek away from his teeth, and shoved the gun muzzle inside of it. Then he began to whisper, obscene, psychopathic threats as to what would happen if Lefty didn't "snap out of it." Presently he removed the gun and asked: "Wha ya say now, soldier?"

"O.K., Sol, O.K."

"Get up."

"O.K., now I'm O.K."

Sol, Bugs, and Lefty walked to the other car, leaving Ben alone. He sat there at the wheel of the car, his lights out, his motor always running, for perhaps ten minutes. Then Sol came back and told him to drive over to Rich Street. At Rich Street they headed out into another drab suburb, and at Reservoir Street Sol said stop. They sat in the dark car a long time now, Sol on the back seat smoking cigars, Ben up front, constantly checking that his motor was running. Some distance away, there was occasionally audible a low mutter, as well as a recurrent scraping noise. The only sign of the strain they were under came when Ben lit a cigarette. Sol savagely ordered him to put it out, not bothering to explain why he could smoke, Ben not. Presently Lefty appeared and got in, and Sol said drive to Ike's, and step on it.

At Ike's Lefty sat alone, in the shadows, drinking beer, and gave no sign that Ben should join him. Ben played pinball, having a small run of luck. Sol sat with Ike and two girls. He was very noisy, very gay.

The sun was coming up as Ben got to his hotel room and dialed the outside phone. "O.K., June, get up. Sorry to rout you out this time of morning, but we got work to do."

"What is it?"

"They've knocked off Arch Rossi and we got to find him."

4

It was after seven, though, before she climbed into his car at Wilkins and Hillcrest; the guard that Ben had insisted on was proving more of a nuisance than a boon, and she had to telephone Jansen before she could shake clear without being followed. They drove first out Memorial, to the spot where Sol had disciplined Lefty, but the only thing in sight was a small toolshed, and it told them nothing. Next they cut over to Rich Street, and drove out to Reservoir, but by daylight, this was just as unpromising. However, across a car track a road construction gang was preparing for work, and she insisted that this must have something to do with their quest. "What makes you think so, June?"

"Why would they come way out here, Caspar and those gunmen of his? There's nothing else to account for it. Whatever they did with him, it had something to do with that road work."

"Such as?"

"Dumping him in that fill, maybe."

"Dumping him—*where?*"

"In that low place there, where they've been filling up to make the road level. They could have driven over there, dropped him off, and then pulled loose dirt over him, anyway enough to cover him up."

"That's no good."

"Why not?"

"It's just not hot, that's all."

"If we could only go over there and *look,* before that gasoline shovel starts piling *more* dirt on top of him."

The shovel was already warming up, giving a quite passable imitation of a battle tank. Ben pulled in his gear, but she touched his arm. "You stay here. *I'm* going over there to see what I can see."

"Look—be careful."

"Don't be so jumpy. Can't I be a naughty little thing? That was parked here last night with my boy friend? And lost my nice wrist watch? Can't I ask them to let me look before they—"

"O.K., but be careful."

She did look a bit like a naughty little thing as she went skipping across the track, in a black dress with a floppy straw hat, and one would have thought the foreman would bow her in with his hat off, wanting to know what he could do for her. He didn't, though. He seemed to be out of humor, and let her stand around while he roared at various workmen. In a few minutes she was back. "What's the matter with him, June?"

"Oh, somebody stole a barrel during the night, and half a sack of cement, and used one of his wheelbarrows for mixing, and—"

At the way his eyes were opening she stopped, stared,

and then started to laugh. "Ben! You don't really mean they'd—put him *in* that barrel, and fill it up with concrete, and—"

"You think they got too much character?"

She got in, and they drove around, cudgeling their brains to think where the hypothetical barrel of concrete, with the just as hypothetical body in it, might have been hidden. She was inclined to minimize the necessity for finding it, but he quickly set her right. "Look, we got to find it, see?—that is, if we're going to lick Caspar. Because he's not licked yet, not the way things are now. You've done fine, you've stirred things up, but it's not enough. Specially since you've made such a play over this kid Rossi. And it won't do any good to say he's dead. They say they never heard of him, and how do you prove your end of it? That's how it is in a court of law, and that's how it is in a political campaign—no body, no murder. We got to find him, see? There's no other dirt that'll do it. Maybe there is, but I don't know any. This is it, or we lose."

They got nowhere that day, though. Around ten o'clock she dropped off, to report to campaign headquarters, and around two Ben reported at the Columbus, as usual. And as usual, these last few days anyway, he and Lefty sat around the big room, reading newspapers, while another procession of visitors went through to the office beyond.

At six Lefty had sandwiches sent up, and at eight Sol came out, while Lefty tuned in the big radio on the speech that Maddux was making in the Civic Auditorium. It was, said the Mayor, the only speech he was making during the campaign, and he would not even have thought it necessary to make that if charges had not been made recently, vicious charges, serious charges, leaving him with no choice but to defend himself. He then reviewed events since the first charges made by "a speaker campaigning for my opponent," with regard to the bandits in the Globe Hotel. But what, he wanted to know, could he have done about that? His opponent did not notify him. Instead, he had called the Castleton police, and these officers had staged one of the most high-handed acts that he, a man many years in public life, had ever heard of. They had come to Lake City, and without one word to Lake City police, or one jot of warrant from a Lake City court, had seized three of the bandits and carried them off.

The fourth, according to the latest charges, had been secreted in the Columbus Hotel. But here again, his opponent, instead of acting in a manner to get lawful results, had preferred making political capital to serving the ends of justice. Instead of offering this information to the Lake City police, he had, through his campaign speaker, screamed it from the rooftops, so that while Lake City police had acted the instant this information came through their radios, they were already too late, the quarry having fled. That is, if there *was* any quarry. Where, the Mayor demanded to know, was this Arch Rossi? On whose word did they have it that an Arch Rossi was mixed up in the Castleton robbery? So far as he was concerned, he was beginning to doubt whether there was such a boy . . .

Nodding exultantly, Sol went back to his office. Lefty listened to the whole speech, then screwed up his face reflectively at the cheers which marked the end of it. "That does it, maybe."

"Does what, Lefty?"

"Settles Jansen's hash."

"Why?"

"When you come right down to it, Arch Rossi was all that really meant trouble. With him out of the way, they can't do much to Sol, or Maddux, or any of them. Well, he's out of the way, boy. A fat chance they'll find him now. And Maddux knows what that means, and so does Sol. He wrote that part of the speech, as a matter of fact. He copied it out this morning and phoned Maddux this afternoon. Oh, yeah—those three in Castleton can talk all they please, but the crime was committed in Castleton, you can't laugh that off. Rossi, of course, he would have been different."

"Looks like we're in."

"Looks like it. Four more years."

Again it was daybreak when Ben got home to his hotel, and he undressed slowly, with pauses while he scratched his head and frowned. Then, when the light was off, he lay there in the gray murk, staring at the ceiling, thinking, concentrating. Then his hand went up in the air, a thick middle finger met thick thumb and hesitated a fraction of a second. Then came the snap, like a pistol shot, and he reached for the phone.

"We're early birds this time, Mr. Grace."

"What time is it, by the way?"

"I have five-thirty."

"O.K., we got the road to ourselves."

"And what is the big idea?"

"*Why* would they put him in a barrel?"

"Now *that,* I can't even imagine."

"I couldn't either, till a half hour ago. I heard about this concrete overcoat, as they call it. But then, when I got to thinking about it, the more I thought the dumber

53

it seemed. I mean, it looked like going out of your way to be crazy, putting yourself to a whole lot of trouble and not getting any advantage out of it. But that's one thing about friend Sol; he never does anything without a reason—unless he gets sore at you or something, and flies off the handle, but even then there's generally something in it for Solly. So I thought and I thought. And the only case I could remember, I don't know if I saw it in movies or read about it in the papers, was a bunch in New York that knocked off a guy and put him in concrete and dropped him in the East River. Does that mean something to you?"

"Not a thing."

"They put him in concrete *to sink him!*"

In the early morning light every grain of powder stood out on her face, and what seemed passably girlish at other times was now woman, squinting at him, trying to guess his meaning. Talking as he drove, he went on: "If it would stay down, there's no place for a body like deep water, is there? But it won't. Pretty soon it's coming up, and ain't that nice? But—imbedded in concrete it'll stay down. Then it's *really* out of sight, and I guess that's why Lefty was bragging to me, how fine this guy was put away."

". . . you mean the lake?"

"It's the only deep water around here."

He spoke with the exultant tone of one who has already solved his problem, but when they arrived at Lake Koquabit they both fell silent, their spirits somewhat dampened. It looked, indeed, quite big; certainly its five miles of length and two of width were sufficiently appalling if Ben had had some idea of dragging the bottom for one barrel of concrete. Slowly they began running past the cat tail marshes on the south shore. Then presently she asked, "How did they get it into the East River?"

"Boat, I think."

"That would be pretty hard here."

"Why?"

"Well—*what* boat?"

"Sol has a boat."

"Is it *big?* Concrete is heavy."

"Big enough. It's a cruiser."

"Where does he keep it?"

"In front of his shack. Moored to a buoy."

"Then they didn't use that. . . . To get it out to the cruiser they'd have had to put it in the rowboat, and that would have been impossible. Or else they would have had to run their car, with the barrel aboard, out on a dock, and run the cruiser around to meet it, and the only dock they could have used would have been the Lakeside Country Club dock, and they'd have run the risk of meeting late poker players, or the watchman, or yacht parties—they simply couldn't have risked it. And besides, they were caught by surprise, from the way you said Lefty acted the other night. They had to get rid of this body in a hurry, and they had no time for a complicated maneuver with a car, a cruiser, and wharf, and I don't know what all."

"So?"

"Maybe they rolled it into the lake direct."

"How?"

"Just push it to the top of a bank and let it go plopping down over the sand. Unless it hit rocks or something it would keep on rolling, even under water, for quite a way. Anyway, until it was out of sight."

"We'll look for marks."

They rode along more purposefully now, their eyes staring at the shore. Once or twice, where the road ran out of sight of the water, she got out and looked, from the top of the bank. But at the end of a mile they had seen nothing, and hadn't even come to a place where a barrel could have been rolled in, considering the problem of the marsh. Then they came to the bridge, and he instinctively pressed the brake, and they looked at each other.

"This is it, Ben. This is where they got rid of it. It was right on their way out from town, and there was no other place. Especially not at night."

To him at least, her confidence didn't seem at all far-fetched. Koquabit, local philologists agreed, came from the Navajo "K'kabe-bik-eeshachi," meaning silver arrow, and this is a fair description of the lake's geography. The lake proper was shaped like an arrow's point, with barbs and all. Making into it was a small lagoon, known as the Inlet, and shaped like the wedge to which the shaft is attached. And Lowry Run, emptying into the inlet, would make a sort of shaft. Connecting inlet and lake was a deep narrows, perhaps two hundred yards across, and it was over this that the bridge ran that they had now come to. It was, as she said, about the only place where a barrel of concrete could be conveniently disposed of, at least by a panicky crew of thugs anxious only to do their work and run.

Ben started over the bridge in low gear, and they both saw the mark at the same time: a white, zig-zagging scratch that would be just about the trail left by a heavy barrel if it were rolled over the concrete parapet. They stopped, counted spans, and then he raced for the end of the bridge, and presently for a side road that forked off the main highway, and made off through the trees.

"You know where you are, June?"

"Haven't the slightest idea."

They had nosed up behind a pleasant shingled house, and stopped, and got out. "This is Solly's shack."

"Oh, my—are we safe?"

"I wouldn't bet on it."

"What are you doing?"

"Throwing off the burglar alarm. That'll help."

He peered under the eaves of a garage, found a switch, and threw it off. Then he led the way, by a narrow board walk, around front, and then down to a boathouse at the water's edge. "What in the world are you up to?"

"You'll see. We got to find that barrel."

Under the rubber mat he found a key, unlocked the little building, and they went inside. At the warm, stuffy smell he started to raise a window, but she stopped him. "I can stand a little heat, even if it's not as fresh as it might be. This morning air has me shivering."

"O.K. Now if you'll turn your back . . ."

"I won't look, but I refuse to go out."

Apparently in completely familiar territory, he took a pair of shorts from a rack, pitched them on a camp chair. Then he began dropping off his clothes, folding them neatly on another chair. In a moment or two he stood stark naked. Then he was in the shorts, finding a pair of canvas shoes to slip on his feet. "You'd better take your coat, Ben."

"Guess that wouldn't hurt."

"While we're paddling over, anyway."

"You handle a canoe?"

"Oh, well enough."

The way she shipped the paddles, however, rolled back the front door, and helped carry the canoe down to the float, indicated she was more expert than she said. When the boat was in the water she had him hold it a moment, while she raced back for the bag of shot she had spied near the camp chairs. "If you're going to be overboard, it'll keep the bow down."

"You better take stern right now."

"All right, you sit forward."

He climbed in the bow, his light overcoat around him, she in the stern. It was less than half a mile, straight across the water, from the shack to the bridge, and it didn't take them long to get there. Presently he slipped his paddle under the strut, caught the abutment, dropped his coat, and stood up.

"You getting out, Ben?"

"Yes."

"Then move the shot bag."

Holding the gunwale, he reached for the bag of shot, caught it, and hefted it forward, clear into the bow. It brought the bow down, but when he stepped on the narrow ledge that ran around the abutment, the boat righted itself. He stood, looking first at the bridge above him, then at the water below, shivering only slightly, managing quite a businesslike air. She swung the boat under the bridge, out of his way and out of sight from above. Then, marking a spot with his eye, he went off.

He was up in a flash, his eyes rolling absurdly, his breath coming in the gasps that only extreme cold can induce. Then a low moan escaped him, and he struck out for the ledge. A stroke or two brought him to it, and he tried to climb out, but couldn't. There were no hand-holds by which he could pull himself up, and not enough space for his body while he drew up his legs. He gave one or two frantic kicks, as though he would throw himself out by main force. Then he turned and lunged for the boat. "Ben! Watch it!"

It wasn't the shriek of a girl afraid of a ducking. It was the low, vibrant command of a woman who re-membered they were half a mile from car and clothes; that a canoe capsized with a bag of shot in the bow would certainly sink; that it would be no trouble for Mr. Caspar to guess what they were doing there; that life thereafter would take on a highly hazardous aspect. Her tone must have reached him, for the hand that was raised to grasp the gunwale didn't grasp it. It slapped back into the water, and he went under, gulping. He came up driving with arms and legs for the shore.

She shot the canoe onto the gravel just ahead of him, stepped to the bow, and jumped out. Seizing his hand, she ran him up and down the beach, until he was a little dry and a little pink, instead of blue. Then she whipped up his overcoat from the bow of the canoe, put it on him, and held it tight against him, her arms around his body. Only then did he begin to talk: a lame, chatter-ing explanation of his sorry performance. It seemed that he had forgotten the peculiarity of the lake, that it remained at an icy temperature until Lowry Run dried up, in July, and the inflow of cold water stopped, giv-ing the sun a chance. However, he said, just let him get his second wind and then he'd go down again.

She listened, and when his shivering stopped they climbed into the canoe and shoved off. They paddled back to the spot they had left and sat silent, he trying to screw up his courage to drop off his coat again and go off. The boat began to shake, shiver, and twist, but he didn't have the curiosity to look and see what she was doing back there. He stared vacantly, first at the sunlight that was now touching the hills back of the shore, then at the water. When the boat went down like an elevator, until the water was within a few inches of the gunwale, he gave a frightened yelp, and only then did he turn his head. The stern was sticking straight up in the air, and she was on the ledge, in pants and brassiere, smiling at him.

"Hadn't you better move aft?"

"Guess that would be a good idea."

She was but a few feet away, and certainly quite an eyeful, but there was no desire in the look he gave her, after he had crawled aft, and adjusted feet, paddle, and coat to the feminine clothes that were draped over the strut. There was only relief; somebody else had taken over his dreadful task. She continued to smile, but checked all details in the boat with her eye, particularly that the shot in the bow made it easily manageable. Only when he was safely settled did she catch the truss above her, chin herself, pull up her feet, and complete the first stage of her climb. Then she reached the top of the parapet and stood there, a pink figurine in the pink morning sunlight, scanning the road for cars. His voice rumbled up, a little peevish: "Look, I'm getting dizzy. If you don't turn around you'll be going over backwards."

"I *am* going over backwards."

"You're—*what?*"

"Well, what's the use of doing a front dive and winding up ten feet further out than I want to get? With a nice back dive I'll half circle around and come right down on the barrel. You haven't forgotten our darling little barrel, have you?"

"*If* you come down on it."

"Oh, I'll come down."

"Little cold down there, you'll notice."

"Oh, for a man, yes."

"Oh, a woman don't feel cold?"

"Not the way a man does, I've noticed it often. I don't care what the weather is, a man's got himself all bundled up in exactly twice as many clothes as a woman wears. Why, look in any street car, and—"

"You haven't forgotten our barrel, have you?"

"Oh, *that*."

A shadow crossed his face, and he looked up to see her in the sky, her arms out, her head back, her back arched in a perfect back dive. Then she floated over, and struck the water with a quick, foamy splash that shot high in the air. She was down a long time; then she came up, with gasps like the gasps that had shaken him. With one hand she pitched a barrel hoop into the canoe, with the other a lump of wet concrete.

"Know what I'm thinking?"

"Look, June, *I'm* thinking. Cut the comedy."

"I'm thinking how funny you looked. When you came up. And you started to snort. And your eyes started to roll. You looked like a wet puppy."

"O.K., so I looked like a puppy."

"A *wet* puppy."

"What's so funny about a wet puppy?"

It had been Ben's turn to shoot the canoe up on the gravel, run the shivering swimmer up and down the shore, and wrap her in a coat. They had taken turns in the boathouse, to dress, and felt a little better when they were back in the car, their clothes on, the motor giving heat. But it wasn't until they got their breakfast that they felt like themselves again. They came to a bar-b-q place, and being afraid to go in together, for fear they might be recognized, they ran a little past it, and Ben went back for hot dogs and pasteboard containers full of scalding hot coffee. Then they ran into a woods, stopped the car, and sat there munching like a pair of wolves. Then she began to talk. He tolerated her kittenishness for a moment or two, but quickly returned to the business in hand.

"What day is today?"

"Saturday."

"You have another meeting tonight?"

"The last of the campaign."

"Where?"

"Municipal Stadium. We were going to have it at Civic Auditorium, but we've been drawing so much bigger crowds lately that we decided to make it a big outdoor rally."

"Then spill it."

"You're sure we found what we were looking for?"

"A barrel don't prove it yet. Maybe somebody else rolled a barrel down there, or one fell overboard while they were building the bridge. But it's as good as we can do, and sooner or later we got to take a chance."

"I was going to, anyway."

"Then I'll call the *Pioneer*."

"Beforehand?"

"Oh, I don't tell them all of it. I just say it's their pal Jack Horner again, and Rossi's body has been found, and you'll tell where at tonight's meeting. It'll build up the crowd."

"So I know what to tell the reporters."

"Let's go."

"*I* said you looked funny."

"Some people got a funny sense of humor."

She reached out with her finger and smoothed the crease between his brows, imitating what he had once or twice done to her. However, he caught her hand and put it aside. "You ought not to be laughing at people. You're an idealist, or supposed to be."

"Can't an idealist think a chiseler looks funny?"

"That don't work."

"It might."

"No."

5

Lights were pleasantly soft in the big room at the Columbus, and humors were high, almost hectic. Sol had visitors: his wife, rather dressed up, and looking a little queer, with her old-world face under a stylish hat; Inspector Cantrell, of the city police, a dapper man in a double-breasted suit; a florid blonde named Irene, in a black satin dress, who had come with the Inspector; and Giulio, a barber. Giulio still wore his white coat, and had come, as a matter of fact, toward the end of the afternoon, to trim Sol's hair. But he had been prevailed upon to stay for dinner and a bellboy had been sent for his accordion; accompanying himself on this, he now gave a series of vocal selections, in a high tenor voice that kept breaking into grace notes. But he would get only two or three numbers sung when Sol would say: "Sing the Miserere," and he would have to launch into *Trovatore,* becoming chorus, soprano, tenor, and orchestra all rolled into one. It is only fair to say that this simplification of the number seemed to improve it.

Ben sat in the shadows, as did Lefty, Bugs, and Goose; they said little and laughed much, as befitted their rank. When eight o'clock came, Lefty tuned in the Municipal Stadium, and cheers came out of the radio, as well as hints by the speakers of disclosures to come. Sol began to clown the discovery of Rossi's body, under the piano, in the radio, behind Giulio's chair. Once, when he yanked open a closet door, Mr. Cantrell's eyes narrowed suddenly at the unmistakable sheen of rifle butts. At each antic the blonde would scream with laughter, say, "Ain't he the limit," and pick up her highball glass. It would be hard to say what lay back of these monkeyshines; whether the whole Rossi question was absurd, whether June was thus due to make a fool of herself, or whether they covered real nervousness. At any rate, Sol was loud, silly, and irritating, for the grins around him were masks. Underneath, these revelers were worried.

Presently, to a volley of comedy from Sol, June was introduced and came on. She took perhaps five minutes on the subject at large, on teamwork, organization, getting voters to the polls next Tuesday, the necessity for electing Mr. Jansen. Then quietly she said she would tell why it was necessary to elect Mr. Jansen, and began to talk about Arch Rossi. She told of her visit that day to Mrs. Rossi, the boy's mother, and to his sister and three little brothers. She told what a good boy he had been, on the testimony of all, until he fell in with the Caspar gang. She told about the Castleton robbery, and the part Arch had played in it, of the way he had been shot, and how he had been brought to the Globe Hotel. She told how he had called up Bob Herndon, and had himself brought to the Columbus, so he could see Caspar, and ask for some decent medical attention.

"Do you know how Caspar answered that plea? Do you know what he did for this poor kid, this nineteen-year-old boy who had helped him get rich, who had kicked in with his share of the $11,000 that Caspar took for so-called 'protection' in Lake City? He took Arch out of the Columbus, for a destination I don't know, because the boy never got there. On the way he was shot and killed. Do you want to know where you can find Arch Rossi now? He's in a barrel of concrete, at the bottom of Koquabit Narrows. I paid a visit to that barrel this morning. I swam down to it, and saw it with my own eyes, between a yellow rowboat that's lying on the bottom, and a white kitten, with a stone tied around its neck, that somebody dropped there to drown. Here's a hoop I took off that barrel, and here's a handful of the concrete!"

It would have been interesting to study a photograph of the scene in the room, as the crowd in the park began to roar, and roar still louder, so that it was several minutes before June could go on. Sol, who had been increasingly comic during the first part of the speech, abruptly fell silent at the words "Koquabit Narrows." Cantrell jumped up and stood listening. Then he looked at Sol, and Lefty looked at Sol, and Goose looked at Sol. In spite of the forecasts in the afternoon papers, something had been said which was wholly unexpected. But Bugs looked at Ben and Ben looked at Bugs; obviously these two didn't know what Sol knew and the other three knew. Giulio and the blonde looked blankly at Mrs. Caspar; just as obviously they were completely in the dark. And Mrs. Caspar looked wearily at the floor, with the ancient dead pan of a woman who knows nothing and can guess all that matters.

"That does it, Solly."

It was Cantrell who spoke, and it was some seconds before Sol looked at him. Then, in a rasping hysterical whine, he said, "Well, come on, let's get out of here! *Le's go, le's go!*"

He grabbed his hat and went lurching out of the room. Mrs. Caspar, seeing cues that would have been invisible to anyone else, got up and followed. Cantrell motioned to the blonde, and they went out. Impatiently, Goose motioned to the barber, who went out like some sort of frightened rabbit, followed by Bugs, and in a moment by Goose and Lefty. Ben, for five minutes or so, was alone. Lighting a cigarette, he smoked reflectively, listening with half an ear to the rest of June's speech, and cutting off the radio when she finished. Once, hearing something, or thinking he heard something, he jumped and wheeled, but there was nothing behind him but the portable bar, with its dirty glasses. He sat down again with the air of a man who is trying to quiet down, to get a grip on himself. When Lefty came in he asked, "What's going on out there?"

"Are you deaf, Ben? Didn't you hear what she said?"

"It was in the papers."

"Not about the Narrows, it wasn't."

"If Sol put him there, why's he surprised?"

"Whatever it is, it's a break for you."

"How?"

"I didn't get no dinner. Let's eat."

Ben walked over, doubled up his fist, brushed Lefty's face with it. "You want that in the kisser?"

"Ben! Let me alone! I've—got the jitters."

"Then talk. How is it a break for me?"

"We been suspicioning you."

"You mean you have."

"O.K., then I have. You bet I have. It's somebody, and I don't know nobody I wouldn't suspicion. O.K., when she said the Narrows, that let you out. No way you could have known about that."

"And what's the idea of Solly's fainting fit?"

"He's not there."

"Who?"

"Rossi! In the Narrows!"

If Lefty noticed Ben's suddenly wide eyes, there was no sign. He sat down, then got up and repeated that he had had no dinner, and "Le's eat." When Ben reminded him they were on duty, he said vaguely that that was right, and then inanely repeated: "Le's eat."

"I don't know about you, but I'm hired to work."

"For who?"

"Caspar, last I heard of it."

"You lug, Caspar's gone."

". . . Where?"

"Where you think? China. Canada. Mexico, maybe. You want to see him, give a listen to the air and a look in the sky. He's on a plane, or will be, soon as him and Maria can wake up that kid, and get him dressed, and hustle him to the airport. I said I'm hungry. Le's eat."

"O.K., pal. Le's eat."

It would be risky, of course, to be too sure about the elements that go into the making of a great American folk drama, such as the arrival of Lindbergh in New York after his flight to Paris, the imprisonment of Floyd Collins in the cave that became his tomb, the celebrations by Brooklyn of the triumphs of its bums.

However, sufficient build-up seems to help, as does an emotional premise that stirs great masses of people, and perfect weather. These things were all present that Sunday afternoon when Sheriff Orcutt, of Lake County, searched Koquabit Narrows for a body, imbedded in concrete. The build-up, to be sure, was rather brief, but of its kind, excellent. It should be remembered that the Narrows was in the county, which had a government all its own, located at Quartz, the county seat, and that as a county Official Sheriff Orcutt was wholly independent of the Caspar-Maddux-Dietz machine that functioned so fearsomely in the city. He was so independent that he had attended, as a matter of legitimate curiosity, the final Jansen rally of the campaign, and had acted on this occasion with true shrieval decision, as Ben would have learned if he had not snapped off the radio so soon.

When June finished speaking he strode majestically to the platform, accompanied by wild yells as the crowd recognized him, divined some exciting purpose, and cheered him. Then he faced Jansen and the crowd, and announced bluntly that if there was any body in Koquabit Narrows he was going to fish it out, and that if they didn't believe him they could all come out there tomorrow afternoon, when he would have divers up from St. Louis, if any were available, and a tow car with a crane, a block, and a falls on it, and a hundred feet of cable.

Thus the newspapers had the story, in ample time for all but their early editions, and that ingredient, the build-up, was taken care of. For the rest, it was Sunday, a circumstance probably not forgotten by the sheriff, who was a bit of a showman himself. And it was a beautiful balmy day, with bees buzzing in the trees, birds twittering in the marshes, and thousands of soldiers free on passes. And there was suspense and sub-suspense of a sort not commonly present on these occasions, created by these agonizing questions: Were divers available, and would they consent to board the sheriff's police plane, not celebrated, exactly, for perfect performance? And, assuming they appeared, would they get the barrel? Would the barrel have Arch Rossi in it? A somewhat ghoulish reek that hung over the project probably didn't diminish its interest; at any rate some 100,000 people gathered to see what could be seen. Their cars were parked along the road at least a mile from each end of the bridge, and their boats were anchored by the dozen, in both lake and inlet. The surrounding hills were black with spectators, as were the shores. Motorcycle police roared back and forth, keeping order and strict lines, and pennants on poles, every twenty or thirty yards, proclaimed ice cream, hot dogs, popcorn, and even lemonade. On the bridge, which was roped off, the sheriff himself was in dramatic command, riding the pinto horse that he used at such festivities, and wearing a ten-gallon hat.

Ben arrived around one-thirty, parked a long way from the bridge, then trudged toward it on foot, along with dozens of others. Profiting by his better knowledge of its topography he turned into a little path that made off from the road, skirted the knolls where most of the spectators were packed, and reached the main abutment at the point where it touched the shore proper. With a quick vault he was on top of it, and sat comfortably down not more than fifty feet from the main theatre of operations. He watched impassively as a plane flew overhead, and people began to call to each other excitedly; as a car arrived, and June, Jansen, and other reform dignitaries stepped out of it; as three other cars arrived, with reporters aboard, and photographers who at once began taking pictures. Once June came quite near, and stood with her back to him, leaning with both elbows against the parapet. He pitched a stone into the water directly beneath her. She didn't turn her head. By this he knew she had already spotted him.

At a roar of approaching motorcycles, he looked around quickly and two officers trotted out to let down the ropes. A truck came through, with two men in undershirts aboard it, and a lot of gear. It crossed the bridge, ran a short distance on the main road, then turned into the side road Ben had taken the preceding morning when he had gone to Caspar's shack. It was intermittently visible through the trees, then ran down on the Lakeshore Country Club dock, where a work boat was waiting. The gear was loaded aboard, and then, as the crowd set up another excited shout, the boat started for the bridge. In a few minutes it arrived, one of the men in undershirts caught an abutment, and a colloquy ensued, between him and June, on the bridge. She pointed directly under her, he nodded, and several police jumped down on the abutment and the one next to it to manage the boat's lines. One of the men in undershirts climbed into a diving suit, the other began to test pump, phones, and cables. A towcar, parked at one end of the bridge, ran out and took position near June, so that its crane, with dangling hook, was just above the spot she had indicated.

The man in the suit was now sitting with his helmet on his knees, his feet hanging over the water, almost ready to go off. There was a hitch, however, when the sheriff climbed down for more pictures, and invited June, Jansen, and the divers to pose with him. This involved persuading a boat to edge in and take the photographers aboard, but presently the thing was done. The subjects of the picture climbed back on the bridge, and the man at the pump put his partner's helmet on, slipped on his earphones. The partner slipped into the water.

In a surprisingly short time, the man with the phones motioned the man on the crane. "O.K., down with your hook." The hook was lowered to him, and he hung cable and clamps over it, and let it go. With a splash it went down in the water, and for perhaps five minutes there was silence, a strained, queer silence as thousands of people waited. Then the man with the phones motioned the man on the crane, and power hit the drum. Jerking a little, like a thin snake, the cable slipped upward. Then the barrel broke water, shedding a shower of drops. It shot upward, dangled for a moment above the parapet, then swung in over the bridge and dropped gently to the roadway. Two policemen stepped forward, with wrenches and sledges. The photographers closed in, making a circle which completely obstructed vision.

There was a delay, as the cable was removed. Then one of the policemen raised his sledge. Ben stood up to see, then climbed to the parapet to see better. The sledge came down. Then it rose and came down again. The cameras began snapping. Then a photographer turned, put his camera under his arm, and came running to Ben's end of the bridge. He didn't jump into the car that had brought him. He ran past it, to a taxi parked in the road. Ducking under the rope and jumping in, he yelled: "The *Post,* and step on it—it's not Arch Rossi, *it's Dick Delany!*"

In utter astonishment Ben's hand went to his brow, and he lost his balance. He teetered perilously for a second or two before he could stoop, jump, and regain his place on the abutment.

"You love me, Ben?"
  "I could try."
  "Turn your mouth around, and try."
  "Hey, I'm driving."
  "Let me drive. I know a place we could go."
  "Your place?"
  "No, a real nice place."
  "O.K., then, the wheel is yours."

It was around ten of the night after election, and they were driving back from Castleton, where they had gone to have dinner, and thus celebrate their victory at the polls. It was the first time they had seen each other since the cold morning at the Narrows, and her amusement at how funny he had looked seemed to have ripened in the interval; her laugh had a tear in its eye and a catch in its throat. A psychiatrist might have found her an interesting study, might have used her, indeed, as an argument against too much innocence in the feminine gender. For no wise lady would have let her affection run wild as June was doing, or at any rate, have let the man see it running wild. She had had a tremendous, grotesque, and dangerous adventure with him that couldn't be denied. Yet this didn't quite account for the way she acted. She gave the impression it was her first contact with such things; that she had never been around much, or if she had, it was by day, to work, and not by night, to play. Certainly she showed no familiarity with the ancient traditions of her sex; she was quite silly, and it was no argument for her performance that after a fashion she was getting away with it. Perhaps Ben too had been around very little. For although he was slightly uncomfortable, occasionally at a loss for an answer to her too-direct sallies, he seemed on the whole to be having a good time. He brought the car to a stop, and let her slide over him to take the wheel, and even pulled her down on his lap for a kiss. When she had the car going again he sat sidewise, to face her, and sometimes lifted her curls with his finger. Presently she said: "Well!"

"Yeah? What's on your mind now?"

"We've been talking all night about what *I* did on election day, and what Mr. Jansen did, and how he hired twenty cars to bring the voters in—let's talk about you. What did you do?"

"Nothing."

"Did you vote?"

"Nope."

"Why not?"

"No civic spirit."

"Why did you help *me?*"

"I told you. Get back at Caspar."

"What did Maddux do?"

"Tried to commit suicide."

"What?"

"They didn't put it in the papers, though I know a couple of those reporters had it. Maybe it wasn't really news. Maybe if he *hadn't* tried to knock himself off, that would have been news. Anyway, he had some kind of pills ready, and when the returns began to come in, he down the hatch with them, and the night gang at the Columbus had an awful time getting him pumped out in time to concede Jansen's election."

"How is the dear old Columbus, by the way?"

"Haven't you been around there?"

"Me? The girl that started it all?"

"You ought to drop in, have a look. Oh, it's perfectly safe. Caspar's gang, you couldn't find one of them with a search-warrant—except Lefty. Lefty, of course, he's a special case. But that hotel, it looks like a morgue. Saturday night, before you went on the air, it was like a bee-hive—politicians, newspaper men, racketeers, women, women, and still more women—everybody you could think of was there, and the orchestra was playing 'Oh Johnny.' Sunday night, after that body was found, it was all over. The night clerk, a cashier, a couple of porters, the bartender—sitting around the bar with me and Lefty, too sick even to have a drink. They knew. They didn't have to wait for any election day."

"Some day I hope to meet Lefty."

"He's scared bad."

"What about?"

"About whether he'll be indicted for the Delany thing. Or something else. About what he's going to do now. About anything else you can think of. Lefty, he's got so he can be scared and not be able to remember what he's scared about. If you ask me, the last two or three stretches did things to him. For that matter, he admits it."

"Caspar is going to be indicted."

"For Delany?"

"Yes. They can't indict him for Rossi. They haven't found any body yet. That's the funniest thing. Here less than a week ago all the town could think of was Rossi, and now everybody seems to have forgotten him."

"Delany's enough. After that, Sol dare not come back."

"What on *earth* did he kill him for?"

"Lefty cleared that up. Delany was an accident. The idea was, they were going to bring him back after he left in his car that day to see his brother in Chicago and write it all up in the *Pioneer*. They were going to bring him back, and hold him somewhere downtown, maybe at the Globe, and then Bill Delany would have to beat it back here, and make a deal, and that would put an end to it, all the stuff that was being pulled. So that's how they started it. Sol put three guys on it, to tail him out of town, and they did it, and about thirty miles out, when he stopped for a light, they closed in on him and one of them took his car and the other two took him, and started back to town with him. But out on Memorial, where they were supposed to switch cars, and Sol was to talk to him before they took him to the hotel, he made a break to get away. And one of Sol's punks let him have it. And that's what Lefty had just found when he came running up to our car that time, and said somebody'd been knocked off, and Sol had to put his knee in his stomach to kick a little wind back in him. I thought it was Rossi, and that was why you and me had the right barrel but the wrong body."

"And they still haven't found Rossi?"

"That's right. He's the big where-is-it."

"What are *you* going to do now, Ben?"

"I hadn't thought."

"Are you in any danger? I mean, like Lefty? Can they indict you? Or try you? For what Caspar was doing?"

"You didn't do anything, you needn't fear anything. As for a job, I'll loaf a few days first."

"Ben, there's one thing."

"Yeah?"

"He's practically given me my pick. I mean, Mr. Jansen has. Of what I want in the way of a city job. And if I were to make a recommendation, he regards my ideas very highly. After what I showed in the campaign. I might—"

"Oh, nuts."

"Why?"

"What would I be doing with a city job? He wouldn't give it to me anyhow. Soon as he found out who I was he'd say he was terribly sorry, he appreciated any help I gave him, but his set-up wouldn't let him do anything for me like that. Then he'd probably offer me a job in his dairy, milking cows. I'm not interested. I don't like him. And I don't need it. I got a little dough saved up. I got *quite* a little."

"I'm kind of proud of you, Ben. It's quite true, what you say. About his probably not being able to do anything about you, even if he wanted to. And another thing, some of these people, these neighborhood people that supported him, might get to talking. They're not very bright at such things. And it might get around *why* you were being taken care of. And you might be on the spot. With some of Caspar's gang. And—there's other reasons."

"O.K.—forget it . . . *Hey!*"

"Look familiar?"

"I'll say."

Her idea of a place to go, it turned out, was Caspar's boathouse, headquarters of the mad quest they had pursued a few mornings before. When she stopped back of the garage, he sat staring at the dark place, then got out, whispering she shouldn't slam her door. They crept around by the board walk, lifted the rubber mat, got the key. Then he turned, stared at the shack itself, put the key back, and motioned to her. Excitedly she followed him. From the top of a shutter he took another key, softly opened the door. They stepped into the dark

77

interior, closed the door behind them, and stood for a time within a few inches of each other. His breath came in tremulous inhalations, perhaps from the reflection that Sol might not have gone to Mexico; that he might have come right here, and laid low, and be holding a gun at this minute in some dark corner before he loosed its crashing, murderous fire.

She whispered: "You scared?"

"Yes."

"Isn't it delicious?"

He caught her in his arms, then felt his head pulled down, as a pair of lips were pressed against his.

He would probably have thought little of all these matters if she had not insisted, around one o'clock that she had to go home, as Mr. Jansen's guard was still on, and would unquestionably report the time of her arrival; and if, after he had dropped her near the apartment in which she lived, he had not passed a parked car of the identical make, year, and color as Mr. Jansen's. He drove by, headed for home. Then suddenly he stopped, got out, and walked back to the other car.

In his little red book he copied the license.

6

He saw her the next night, the night after that, and the night after that. She continued to act with that complete abandon of a novice having her first drink, and yet, when he suggested dinner at the Savoy Grill, she preferred Castleton; when he wanted to linger longer at the shack, she had to get home; when she dropped off at a corner, pleading an errand at a drug store, he found the green car, parked half a block away. His manner, these three evenings, changed just a little. He didn't exactly resist her; he would hardly have been human if he had, considering the inducements. But he was not quite so oafishly pleased, not so completely at a loss for replies. They were a little flat, perhaps, but they were articulate, and quite coolly considered. And constantly he studied her, as though he were trying to make up his mind about something, or to figure out something, into which she definitely fitted.

Sunday night her high spirits had vanished, and she was glum, sad-eyed, clingy. Some men would have been bored, but he studied her more narrowly than ever, and patted her with tender sympathy. In the shack she broke down completely. They didn't dare burn electricity here, but they had become sufficiently bold as to light a candle, and stick it to the floor, in front of the sofa in the living room. By this murky light her eyes glittered as she sobbed, and when he gathered her in his arms, and whispered in her ear, she quieted down, pulled herself together, and began to talk. "It's the same old thing, Ben."

"Family?"

"Not my whole family. Just my—sister."

"She the one that causes that frown you got?"

"Ever since I can remember I've had to think about her, worry about her, get her out of messes. She's all right, Ben. She's the sweetest kid you ever saw, but— she's always in trouble. And it's always me that has to get her out."

"She younger than you?"

"Three years. She's twenty-two."

"What's she done this time?"

"Well, you see, she's in college, and—"

"You pay for her there?"

"Pretty near all."

"That's why you can't keep all you make?"

"Yes, of course."

"Go on."

"So, she has a room-mate—a girl I never did like— and this girl took some things. From other girls, in the dormitories. And Dorothy had no more sense than to let her store them in the room. In a trunk. And—then day before yesterday the room was searched. And the things were found. And—"

"The cops got her, hey?"

"No, it's not that bad, yet. Nobody wants to prosecute. But yesterday a lot of the things were traced, and this girl, Dorothy's room-mate, has to pay for them, or else."

"How much does it tote?"

"Over two hundred dollars."

"Quite a lot of dough."

"And I don't know what I'm going to do."

Ben got up, lit a cigarette, flicked the match into the fireplace, and stood facing her. For a time he smoked, eyeing her steadily. Then: "I don't see why you're taking it so hard. Two hundred bucks, sure that's a lot of money. But you can get it easy enough."

"Where?"

"Jansen."

"No, I couldn't do that."

"Why not?"

"Oh—I couldn't go to him, that's all. He—he's going to make me Chief of Social Service, and I can't ask for more than that. I could pay it out of my salary, if I only had time. But my first pay check will be in August, and if I don't make this thing good she'll be put in jail, and—"

"You sure that's why you can't go to Jansen?"

"Of course it is."

"You're not stuck on him, by any chance?"

". . . *You!* Can ask *that!*"

"Sure. Why not?"

"I don't even know what you mean."

"No? That first night we were out together, you had

to leave here because the guards were at your place, and they'd tell Jansen what time you came in. But Jansen's car was outside, and Jansen was downstairs waiting for you. He was there Thursday night, and Friday night, and last night. Each night he stayed over an hour. What are you trying to do, kid me? I say you're stuck on him."

He was cold, but not particularly indignant. From his manner, one might think he was playing a carefully rehearsed scene. She shook her head emphatically. "No, you're wrong, though I can see why you think what you do. I'm not stuck on him. And—he has no personal interest in me. It was business, things we had to talk over. He's married, and—"

"His wife's in a sanitorium."

"I wouldn't know. I—"

"No? I'd imagine he'd have quite a lot to say about that wife, how long she's been in the sanitorium, how sick she is all the time, how much he loves her, how much it means to him that he has somebody he can tell about her, and that understands how he feels. If you're not stuck on him, it certainly looks like he's stuck on you. It looks—"

"All right, then, but if somebody got stuck on me, I'd certainly not go and tell anybody. You, or anybody."

"Then O.K."

"And I'd never go and ask them for—"

"Then O.K. . . . . There's other places to get dough."

"Where?"

She was eager, but he took his time about answering, lit another cigarette, flicked another match into the fireplace. "Well, me for instance."

"You? Would you let me have two hundred dollars?"

"I got two hundred. I got two thousand."

"Why couldn't you have made this offer without all these ugly insinuations about me and Mr. Jansen?"

"I got to know where I stand."

"Yes, of course he likes me. He—likes me a lot. He *ought* to, after all I've done for him. But—honestly, Ben, I just hate it that you stood out there and—"

"Can't a guy be jealous?"

He didn't look jealous. He looked like a man who had thought up something he was sure would score. It did. She drew breath to say something, then got up, put her arms around him, looked him in the eye, and kissed him exaltedly on the mouth. "I think that's one of the sweetest things I ever had said to me. I—just love you for that."

"What she do it for?"

"Who? That girl?"

"Yeah, Dorothy."

"It was the room-mate, Ben. She—"

"Hey, hey."

"All right, there isn't any room-mate. Are you really going to let me have the money?"

"Sure. How much is it?"

"Two twenty. And the wire charges."

"You'll have it. Tomorrow morning. By the way—"

"Yes?"

"Is Jansen going to be there tonight?"

"Not if you object."

"Oh, I don't object."

"That's right. There's nothing to be jealous of."

"You could ask him a favor, though."

"Anything you say."

"Ask him to appoint Cantrell Chief of Police."

"Appoint—whom did you say?"

"You heard me."

They had been standing in front of the fireplace, she snuggling against him, he patting her on the shoulders. Now he walked over and sat down near the candle, so its light shone upwards on his face as he looked at her. It gave him a curiously wolflike look. She stared, then came over and sat beside him. "Ben, what on earth are you talking about?"

"Cantrell."

"But he's a dirty crook. Why, he—was hand in glove with Caspar. Why, Ben, *how* could Jansen appoint him? It would make a laughing stock of the whole campaign."

"If Jansen really wants to appoint the best available man, and goes into the qualifications of them all, he'll find that Cantrell is the best officer on the force. It's not his fault if crooks get elected and he has to play along. Give Cantrell a break, and he's one of the best officers in the country. And a good officer Jansen will have to have, if he's going to put across what he's been promising the voters. He can't deliver with jerks and thugs."

"He can't appoint Cantrell."

"O.K."

He yawned, coldly and indifferently. "You mind if we blow along now? I been thinking about it, and I think I better be making an early start over to Castleton, start looking for a job."

"How early?"

"Ah, seven, eight o'clock probably."

"Before the bank opens?"

"Oh yeah, long before that."

She sat a long time looking at him, her face wearing a look of pain. "I guess I see it now, Ben. What this is all about. Why you've been acting just a little peculiarly these last few days."

"Yeah? Why is that?"

"Once you found out that Jansen was insanely in love with me, you knew, or thought, you had him, didn't you? That through me you could make him do whatever you wanted him to do, even to appointing that filthy swine, Cantrell. And tonight, when you heard about Dorothy, you saw something that played right into your hand, didn't you?"

"I haven't asked for a thing in this campaign."

"That's right. You were satisfied just to get Caspar, and be a free man once more. But the Jansen angle—I don't have any idea how you found out about it. You seem to have a habit of finding out things, and thinking up schemes. But when you did find out about it, you decided to use it for your own ends, didn't you? Just as you used what you knew about Caspar—"

"So did you. Don't forget that."

"I wasn't working for him."

Ben got up, picked up the candle, blew it out. In the dark there was a long pause. Then he said, "Just one more thing about Cantrell—"

"No, not even one thing. I know what you can do if you can get Cantrell made Chief of Police. You can run this town exactly as Caspar did. Well, you won't, that's all. He'll not be appointed."

"O.K. Sorry about Dorothy."

". . . Never mind—about Dorothy."

Lefty materialized from a shadow when Ben headed into the parking shed, and walked with him into the hotel and up to his room. He wanted to borrow $5. Ben let him have it, and lay down on the bed. He lay there a long time, his eyes on the ceiling, listening to Lefty's downhearted view of the future. He was preoccupied, as though he were waiting for something. When the outside phone rang he stiffened a little, reached for it, then changed his mind. It rang a great many times, until Lefty became annoyed, and wanted to know why he didn't answer. When it stopped, Ben abruptly sat up. "Lefty, how much did Sol pay you?"

"Eighteen."

"What—a week?"

"O.K., then laugh, let's see you laugh. For all I did, taking a chance on my neck every other day—he paid me eighteen a week and I took it, that's the funny part. For something special he slipped me extra."

"You can start tomorrow at twenty-five."

"Who from?"

"From now on I'm running it."

". . . Ah, so it *was* you!"

"So what?"

"Not a thing. I got not a word to say."

"Pals?"

"Two beers, Ben, and they're on you."

7

Inspector Cantrell raised his eyes as Ben came in, motioned vaguely to a chair, went on reading. In his manufacture, one would say that God had started with the feet, shaping them delicately; then proceeded to the body, making it strong and at the same time supple, not too large and not too small; then reached the head as the whistle blew for lunch. It was a round, bulletlike head, on the front of which a face had indeed been moulded, but a face hastily conceived, whose component parts didn't noticeably match; the heavy jaw was out of kilter with the narrow, low forehead; the right side was seamy, the left side not; it was even somewhat out of plumb, skewing off at an angle in a baffling way. Yet its dark mahogany color gave a startling, sharklike vividness to the light blue eyes, so that while one might instinctively avoid Mr. Cantrell, one would hardly trifle with him. He was, at this moment, taking his ease after lunch. His feet rested comfortably on the desk, his knee cradled a magazine. Under his chin, a light blue handkerchief protected a dark blue shirt, and behind him, a hanger spread his double-breasted coat. He wore no waistcoat. His belt, as it rose and fell with his regular breathing, was held by a monogrammed clasp.

Presently he yawned, pitched the magazine aside, clasped his hands behind his head. "Well, Ben, what do you know?"

"Not a thing, Joe."

"Me neither. Things awful slow. What you doing?"

"Nothing yet."

"You hear from Sol?"

"No, nobody does."

"Sol, when he skipped he skipped high."

"He going to be indicted?"

"You couldn't prove it by me. You wouldn't hardly expect him to be, many friends as he's got right now in the D.A.'s office. But when this new gang comes in, I don't know. I wouldn't put much past them."

"When's the new outfit come in?"

"Week from tomorrow."

"Gee, time sure does fly, don't it?"

"Sure does. Well, Ben, what's on your mind?"

"Who's the new chief?"

"Search me."

"O.K., stand up."

". . . *What?*"

"I say come over here and back up. I might be able to find a card or a letter or something with the name of Cantrell on it."

Mr. Cantrell smiled the smile of one who wants to be polite in the presence of the feeble-minded. "No, Ben, sometime your number's up and sometime it's not. For the next four years I imagine I got outside position."

"Suppose they disqualified the winner, the place horse, the show horse, and the horse that was trailing them, and you saw your number going up to the top—what then?"

"They don't often do that."

"Not in a straight race."

"I figure this one's not fixed—for me, anyway."

"Suppose you're wrong."

"It's too hot for supposing. What you want, Ben?"

"Take your feet off that desk."

". . . Says who?"

"You think I came in here to crack jokes?"

There was quite a change in Ben's manner since the last time Mr. Cantrell had seen him. Then he had been a face in the shadows of Sol's big room, grinning appreciation of barbers, blondes, and cops; now he was callous, calm, and cold. How much of this was real, how much was an imitation of Caspar, and how much was play-acting, to bring Cantrell to heel, it would be hard to say. Possibly it involved all three, and yet it wasn't all bluff. Ben evidently felt a great sense of power, an intoxicating sense of power. He lit a cigarette, walked over, dropped it into the constabular ashtray, and stood looking at Mr. Cantrell's feet, as though they were almost more than his patience could endure.

Mr. Cantrell stared for some time, then said: "If my feet bother you, Ben, I can take them down. I can treat you with courtesy, or hope I can. But I don't take them down, for you or anybody, or any such say-so as that."

"If you don't mind, Joe. I ought to have said that."

"That's a whole lot better."

89

"You ready to suppose?"

"That all depends, and I got to know a lot more about it first. But you can get this straight, right now: I don't take anything, off you or anybody. I didn't even take it off Caspar. You did, Ben, but I didn't."

At this reminder of the lowly role he had played, Ben's eyes flickered. Obviously he would have liked to let the thing rest there, to let Mr. Cantrell have his dignity, to get on with the deal. It would be less trouble that way, and he hated trouble. But something must have told him this was really a test of strength, that if he weakened now, he couldn't handle this man, even if he bagged him. He smiled pityingly. "So you never took it off Caspar, hey? It's a good thing he's not here to hear you say that. Now you know and I know and we all know that if you stuck around Caspar you took it or you didn't stick. I notice you were there, right up to the last whistle blow, and that means you took it. So that's what you're doing now."

His big halfback's paw hit Mr. Cantrell's feet, which were still on the desk, and Mr. Cantrell's feet hit the deck. Mr. Cantrell came up standing, then walked around the desk, and the two men faced each other malevolently. Then Mr. Cantrell's face wrinkled into a grin, and he nudged Ben in the ribs. "Hey, Ben, you forgot something."

"Yeah, and what's that?"

"It's not the heat makes me like this, it's—"

"The humidity?"

"Right!"

Both roared at this sally, in a room-shaking, tension-easing laugh, and Mr. Cantrell felt in Ben's pockets for a cigarette. "Were we supposing, Ben?"

"That's it, copper."

"Go on, tell me some more."

"If you want to be Chief, I might swing it."

"You in person?"

"Yeah, me."

"You and Jansen; I didn't know you were that thick."

"We're not."

"O.K., just getting it straight."

"Just the same, I can swing it."

"Keep right on."

"Of course, you got to sell him. You got to convince him that you, or any cop, can clean this town up in twenty-four hours, providing one thing."

"Which is?"

"You get a free hand."

"And then?"

"Surprise, copper, surprise! Then you clean it."

"A clean tooth don't grow much fat."

"You follow the chickens?"

"Yeah, a little."

"O.K., then you know how they cut off the spur, just a little way from the foot. And you know how they fit that gaff over the stump—that pretty-looking thing that's all hand-forged steel, with a point on it that would go through sheet-iron, and a nice leather band to go around his leg, soft, so it don't hurt him any, and he likes it . . . So you clean up the town, you do it for Jansen, just like you said you would. You cut off the spur, and that cleans it. How can a chicken violate the law with no spur to fight with? O.K., you just don't tell him about that gaff in your pocket, that's all. You got it now?"

"No."

"Well, you will."

"Look, smart guy, what do I *do?*"

91

"Do? You do nothing, You get called in, that's all. You and about twenty others, one at a time you get called in to say what you got to say, if anything. And you, you got nothing to say. Sure, you can clean the town up. Any cop can—providing you get a free hand. You don't polish apples, you don't shake his hand, you don't even care. But you mean business, if he does."

"Well, *does* he?"

"He appoints you acting chief."

"And?"

"Then you hit it. Then you're in."

"Boy, it's clear as mud."

"Oh, mud settles if you give it time."

A half hour later, in another place, where he could be friendly and frank, Ben was more natural, seemed to be having a better time. This was in the office of Bleeker & Yates, a firm of lawyers in the Coolidge Building, whereof the senior partner, Mr. Oliver Hedge Bleeker, had just been elected District Attorney by a majority as big as Mr. Jansen's. So it was with Mr. Yates, the junior partner, that Ben had his little visit. He was a graying man in his thirties, and kept his blue coat on, as befitted an attorney with an air-conditioned office. Ben took him completely, or almost as completely, into his confidence, and made no secret of his former connection with Caspar. But he hastened to explain the circumstances: the abdominal injury, received in professional football; the need of work, and the offer from Caspar; then the absurd situation that developed, wherein his distaste for the job collided with the unpleasant probability that if he quit it he would be killed, for what he knew, and to gratify Caspar's conceit. As Mr. Yates' eyes widened, Ben went on, telling of his activities for Jansen. He didn't say what they were, and insinuated they were pathetically slight. Yet he insisted he had been a Jansen man. "I just about got to the point where if I couldn't call my soul my own I was going to call my *carcass* my own. Yes, I worked for Jansen, and I'm proud of it. I want you to know it, because before we go any further you'd better know the kind of guy I am."

"Were you the—'leak-spot,' as we called it?"

"The what?"

"Well—Miss Lyons, as I suppose you know, had a source of information about Caspar. In the Jansen organization, we never knew exactly who that source was, as she never told us. We always called it the 'leak-spot.' "

"I can't tell you the source of Miss Lyons' information. I played a small part in the campaign. It was small, and believe me it was unimportant. But I'd like you to know I was against Caspar, I was helping to break him, before now. During the campaign. While it was still a fight."

"And what do you want with me?"

"You know anything about pinball?"

"Why, I've played it, I guess."

"I mean the hook-up."

"Well, not exactly."

"You reform guys, you don't know much, do you?"

"Well, is it important?"

"Look, I can't tell you from way-back, but in my time there's been just two rackets. Two really good ones. Two rackets that made money, and kept on making it, and were safe—or safe as a racket ever gets. One was beer, until prohibition got repealed, and the other is pinball, and both for the same reason. You know what that reason is?"

"Human greed, I suppose."

"No—human decency."

"I don't quite follow you."

"Beer—I don't talk about hard liquor, because that was really intoxicating—but *beer,* that was against the law mainly because the great American public thought it was, well, you know, a little—"

"Scandalous?"

"That's it. But once they went on record about it, they didn't really care. It was just a little bit against the law, if you know what I mean. That meant it was just as illegal as some D.A., or enforcement officer, or maybe both of them working together, said it was. That meant you could make a deal. Not all over, maybe, but most places. You remember about that?"

"Oh yes, quite vividly."

"O.K., then beer went, didn't it?"

"You mean it became legal?"

"That's it—anybody could sell it, and the racket went. So the boys had to find something. So for a while they made a mess of it. They tried stick-ups, and kidnapping, and Murder, Inc., and a lot of stuff that didn't pay and that landed plenty of them in the big house and quite a few on the thirteen steps. And then they got wise to gambling. Of course, that wasn't exactly new."

"I wouldn't think so."

"No, that cigar-store front with a bookie behind, and that guy on the corner, selling tickets to a policy game, and the big bookie places downtown—most of that had been going on a long time. But beer, when it made its comeback in the drug stores and markets and groceries, that gave the boys an idea. Why not put gambling in the drug store too? Why not bring it right to the home, so Susie and Willie and Cousin Johnny can drop their nickel in the slot? And when they went into it a little they found out that pinball was like beer. The great American public frowned on it, but didn't really care. It was against the law, but not very much. So that meant they could make a deal. So they did. And all over the United States you'll find these machines, in drug stores, cafes, ice cream parlors, bowling alleys, and restaurants. They're outlawed in New York now, and Los Angeles, and a few other places, but everywhere else, they're wide open."

"Wait a minute, you're going too fast for me."

"Yeah? What's bothering you?"

"Who owns these machines, Mr. Grace?"

"O.K., now I'll give it all to you, quick. You understand, anybody can make amusement machines, and plenty of them are made locally—juke boxes, shovel games, pinball, whatever you want. They're made in those little tumbledown places over on the other side of the carline, where you wouldn't hardly believe there'd be a factory at all. But most of them, the good ones, with shiny gadgets on them and patent attachments, come from Chicago. That's the center, and two or three of the big houses there make ninety percent of the national product. Some of them are O.K. The juke boxes, for instance, they're not against the law anywhere, and they got good tone quality if you like tone. I don't."

"Me neither."

"But the rest, the pinball machines, no manufacturer in Chicago takes a chance on what some D.A. is going to do. They've got to be owned locally, and they've got to be paid for in cash. In Lake City, they're owned by about the sickest bunch of jerks you ever saw—stooges for Caspar, that could scrape together a few hundred dollars to buy some machines, and that had to scrape it together, for one reason or another. Then they were set. They had their machines, and they gave him his cut, and the machines paid, clear of the fifty percent to the drug store man, and Solly's cut, and one or two other little rake-offs we've had, three or four bucks a month to the owner. That meant that in a year he had his money back and the rest of it was gravy. The drug store man, he was sitting pretty. He had two or three machines in, and they paid seven-eight-nine bucks a month apiece, and that was a good slice of the rent. And it was cash. And—"

"It's *still* going on, isn't it?"

Ben, who had been striding around, giving Mr. Yates the benefit of his researches and reflections for the last few weeks, sat down now with a cryptic smile. "As to that, suppose *you* tell *me*."

"I—what would I know about it?"

"They're still going, of course, but whether they'll be going, or what the situation is going to be after the new administration goes in—that depends pretty much on your partner, Mr. Bleeker, the new D.A."

"I can't tell you what he's going to do."

Mr. Yates spoke quickly, sternly, conscientiously. Ben shrugged amiably. "Just gagging. None of my business what he's going to do, but—"

"Once more: What do you want with *me?*"

"Oh, I'm coming to that. Now, Mr. Yates, I'm going to surprise you. So far as Lake City is concerned, *I* believe pinball is doomed."

"Why?"

"Because it's wrong. To the extent that it's gambling,

it's wrong, and that temptation ought to be taken away from our young people, and if I know your partner, Mr. Yates—of course I can only judge from the speeches he made in the campaign, but he made himself pretty clear—he's going to take that temptation away. I'm betting my money that that's the way the cat is going to jump, and that's why I've come in to see you."

"Yes, I'm listening, Mr. Grace."

"To the extent that it's a game of chance, it's wrong, and that part is against the law. But to the extent that it's a game of skill, it's good clean recreation, and that's *not* against the law."

"Just how do you separate these two aspects of pinball—or is that metaphysical operation supposed to be *my* useful function?"

Mr. Yates' tone was dry, his expression ironical, his eye cold and steely. Ben jumped up and gave him a little, just a little, of the manner he had turned on Mr. Cantrell.

"Listen, pal, I didn't come in to ask you to turn black into white, or whatever you mean by that crack about metaphysics. I've come in to offer you a perfectly legitimate and honest and decent job, so let me finish before you crack smart . . . I separate them, by using different machines, a completely different class of amusement equipment. Those companies in Chicago, they haven't been asleep either, brother. They can read the writing on the wall just as well as I can. The law, it's pretty much the same in every city of the country, and it prohibits a game of chance. A game of chance, with a pay-off, is out, and they know it. Understand, this is local legislation all over the country, but one by one, communities are going to put that game of chance on the skids. But those kids, and those drug stores, between them, they've developed a demand for a decent, honest game of skill—baseball, football, softball, all sorts of table imitations of the big stuff outside, that kids can play with each other at night, have a good time, and not lose every dime they've got. There's no pay-off. Have you got that? *There's no pay-off.*"

"I think you make that clear."

"The most those kids get is a certificate, or engraved diploma, whatever it is, saying they made a home run, or hole-in-one, or dropkick from the fifty-yard line, just a souvenir, because experience shows you've got to give them *something,* or the game don't pay. But, experience also shows that this class of game is just as profitable, to the drug store owner, as gambling—"

"How can it be?"

"They enjoy it better. They play each other, not the machine, so it's all on the up-and-up. They get a break. That's what cuts the machine's take on gambling pinball: those kids wake up, sooner or later, that they're being cheated. This way they're not."

"Now I've got it. Go on."

"All right, so I've got a hook-up, I've got it arranged to bring in this new class of machine and install them in Lake City—if, as, and when the old ones are thrown out. I don't know what Mr. Bleeker is going to do, and I don't ask you even to ask him what he's going to do. But this much I've got to know: Is my class of machine legal? I can't take a chance on bringing in five thousand machines here—"

"Five *thousand?*"

"Look—there's five hundred drug stores around Lake City, two or three hundred cafes, I don't know how many ice cream parlors—I'm trying to get it through your head that this is *big business*. I can't take a chance on that much dough, and then have friend Bleeker decide that the felt on the table don't meet the requirements of Section 492 of the Sanitary Code, something like that. I've got to know where I stand, and I've got to know in black and white. That's the first thing. You know him, and you can certainly put a legal question to him that he's bound, as I see it, to answer. The next thing is, just to protect the interest of all the little guys that want to put machines in, I'm going to organize an association. I don't kid you about it. That association is going to know from the beginning that it's politically powerful. It's got two or three men in key spots of every precinct, and it can make any D.A., whether his name is Bleeker or whatever it is, treat it polite, with no kicking around. I want you to represent that association, as attorney. For that, you'll receive a pretty nice yearly retainer. Just how much I don't know today, but we can work it out. I don't ask you to do anything but represent us legally—but we want real representation, and you look to me like you've got some stuff. I don't mind saying I've had my eye on you since before the election. Well—now you know where *you* come in, at last."

Mr. Yates got up and took several turns about his office. Presently he sat down. "Well—there's a little question of ethics here."

"I don't quite know what you mean."

"You see, I'm Bleeker's partner."

"That's O.K. by me."

"I'm not sure it is by me. Or—by the bar association. Or—by Mr. Bleeker. I'd say it was one of those things—"

"Well, if the ethics bothers you I can go somewhere

99

else and no hard feelings. I came in here, as I told you, because—"

"Hey, wait a minute."

"O.K. Sorry."

"I haven't turned your offer down. But I *would* like to think it over a bit. Perhaps talk to Mr. Bleeker about it. See what *he* thinks of the propriety of my accepting such a—"

"Now I get it."

"Shall we meet again—say next week?"

"Next week is fine."

So it happened, some days after Mr. Jansen's inauguration, that a throng of frightened druggists, cafe owners, and other such people, assembled in one of the convention rooms of the Hotel Fremont. It had been, indeed, a somewhat disturbing week. First of all, there was the alarming circumstance that Mr. Jansen, the afternoon he took office, appointed a police board of three of the leading reformers of the town. Two days later this board had named Joseph P. Cantrell as acting Chief, and for a brief time there was a false dawn, a hope that Mr. Jansen wasn't quite so stern as he had pretended. Then, in quick succession, came two occurrences that had nothing to do with Mr. Jansen, but which didn't harmonize, somehow, with an easy view of life. The Federal grand jury indicted Mr. Caspar for certain violations of the income tax law. Then the county grand jury indicted him for the murder of Richard Delany. Then, after these straws blowing down the wind, the tornado struck. A uniformed patrolman, one afternoon, entered every place in the city where pinball machines were in operation, and stood guard over them until a truck appeared outside, and expert workmen came in, took the machines apart, and stowed them in the truck. After the truck had departed, to the wail of sirens, the uniformed patrolman left a summons with the owner, notifying him to appear in police court next day and defend himself against preposterous charges: the maintenance of a nuisance, the maintenance of devices tending to the corruption of minors, the operation of common gambling machines.

Then next morning had come the postcard that might mean an answer to all these bewildering things: it was signed by Benjamin L. Grace, and simply informed the recipient that a meeting of the Lake City Amusement Device Operators' Association would be held that day at the Fremont, and that any operator of an amusement machine would be eligible to attend. The time of the meeting, 2 P.M., had been set, obviously, with an eye to the time of the hearings, which were to be in the Hall of Justice Building at four o'clock. By 1:30, worried little men in gray mohair coats began to appear at the Fremont, to be led by a bellboy to Ballroom A, where they sat down in groups to whisper, and wait for whatever was forthcoming. Ballroom A had been furnished by the hotel as an accommodation to Ben, who was living there now, in one of the Sky-Vista apartments, consisting of living room, bedroom, bath, and pantribar alcove. Of the better hotels in Lake City, the Fremont was the oldest, and the most serious rival of the Columbus.

By two o'clock, Ballroom A was a beehive, with every folding chair occupied, and people standing in the aisles. Ben entered with Mr. Yates, who sat down at the table which had been placed at one end of the room. Ben didn't sit. He faced the crowd, rapped them to order with a large glass ashtray, and asked somebody near the doors to close them. He had changed perceptibly, even since the interview with Mr. Yates, and enormously since that day when a sniveling chauffeur had told his woes to Lefty. Yet there was something of that chauffeur in him now, as he threw back his shoulders and began to talk in quick, jerky, confident sentences. Perhaps it was his inability, in spite of his effort to do so, to give more than the meanest of assurances to this crowd, who were nervous about today, and worried about tomorrow. He tried to be lofty, to appeal to their civic spirit, or pride in their establishments, or something of the sort, as he told them what he had told Mr. Yates about the association and the new class of machine which he would make available to members; and yet somehow he sounded like a professional football coach, haranguing his men before a game, and barking, rather than talking.

Fortunately, however, it was an occasion where sense counted more than manner. They listened to him intently. When, coming to the question of membership, he borrowed a device from June and broke open a package of slips, they sprang forward, those on the front row, to help him distribute them, and when they had been filled out, to collect them and pile them on the table. Practically everybody, it seemed, wanted to be a member, to be supplied with the new type of machine, to be represented in court by Mr. Yates, to pay a moderate assessment, which would be collected only from the earnings of the machines.

Ben spoke perhaps twenty minutes, the formalities with the slips took another twenty, and then there were quite a few questions.

Then Mr. Yates took the floor. "Before we leave here to appear in court, I'd like to make my position clear.

I represent association members and association members only. But any others, and any members who want to appear individually, with different counsel or with no counsel, are welcome to do so, and will merely have to ask the court that their cases be disjoined, and they'll have separate trial. Now just to get straight whom I represent and whom I don't will those who want separate trials please raise their hands?"

There were no hands.

"Very well, then I take it I represent you all. Now this isn't binding on you, but my advice is that when your case is called—whichever one of you happens to be called first as a sort of test case—you plead guilty. I can then ask the court to let me put into evidence, before it imposes sentence, the circumstances that attended the installation of these machines, the pressure from the Caspar organization, the intimidation, the 'heat,' as they say, that was turned on, and that ought to have great weight with the court in fixing the degree of guilt. There may be a small fine. If so, it will be credited to you, against the dues of the association—in other words you will have to pay the fine today, in cash, but the association will reimburse you. Now are there any questions?"

There weren't any, and a half hour later the throng was in Magistrate Himmelhaber's courtroom, filling it to the last row of benches, and streaming out into the hall and down the marble staircase into the lobby of the Hall of Justice. The police sergeant's voice sounded small and queer as he read the charges, and started to read the names, but Mr. Himmelhaber stopped him.

"Call the first case."

"Roscoe Darnat."

"Here."

"Roscoe Darnat, you are charged with the maintenance of a nuisance, in violation of Section 448 of the—"

"Dismiss it."

Mr. Himmelhaber looked a little annoyed, motioned to the sergeant. "Dismiss all those funny ones, try him on gambling charges only."

"Yes, Judge. Roscoe Darnat, you are charged with the operation of games of chance, on or about your premises at 3321 West Distler Avenue, on July 7 and various dates previous thereto—are you guilty or not guilty?"

"Guilty."

Mr. Himmelhaber leaned forward with interest, looked at Mr. Yates. "Are they all taking a plea?"

"Yes, your honor. I would like the court to hear a little testimony on the pressure that was put on them to let the games come into their establishments, as establishing extenuating circumstances—"

"O.K."

Led by Mr. Yates, with occasional questions from the magistrate, Mr. Darnat told his harrowing tale, of how under pressure from Mr. Caspar's lieutenants he had installed one machine; of how, after downright intimidation, he had accepted another; of how, when he was afraid for the lives of his wife and children, he had accepted a third and a fourth; of how he asked only to be clear of gambling in any form; how he actually threw up his hat and cheered, if the Judge didn't believe it he could ask his wife, when the truck carried off the four machines—"

"O.K., that's enough."

Mr. Himmelhaber looked at Mr. Bleeker, who was

prosecuting the case in person, and who had said nothing so far. He looked over his glasses at the judge, said: "Your honor, I have no questions to ask the witness. In fact, I'm sure that every word he says is true. . . . I may say, to make the position of the prosecution clear, that I have no desire to harry these people, or inflict undue hardship. If they were actually the owners of the machines, that would be different. But since no owners have come forward to claim their property— quite naturally, I would say—what I am interested in is the destruction of the machines, so that the nuisance they represent can be abated, for good and all."

Mr. Himmelhaber looked at Mr. Yates. "That's all right with me, your honor. My clients, so far as I know, don't own a single machine."

"Then, sergeant, will you write the order?"

"I got it already wrote."

In the old Ninth Street station house, not used since the erection of the Belle Haven building further out, the machines had been stored pending court order for their disposal, and thither, around eight that night, flocked the photographers who had snapped the throng in the Hall of Justice. They were to take pictures of an ancient constabular rite: the destruction of equipment seized in a gambling raid. The attorneys were not there for the occasion, but Mr. Cantrell was, dressed in a neat pinstripe, with a white carnation in his buttonhole. His hair was rather specially combed, as was the hair of various officers, who opened the front door for the cameramen, and consulted with them as to the scene of the ceremony.

The big front room, with the old sergeant's desk in it, seemed the only likely place, as the rest of the building was jammed with equipment to be destroyed. So the pitch was made there, and the police, with unusual courtesy, helped adjust lights, set up cameras, and pick out the most colorful equipment. Then two of them stepped forward, armed with axes. Then Mr. Cantrell was posed, and warned not to smile, as it was a solemn occasion. Then various prominent detectives were posed, in the background, to be "looking on," in the picture caption, later. Then the cameras began to shoot. Amid frantic cries of "Hold it," "One more," "Don't drop that axe yet," and so on, several more shots were made, and then abruptly, with scarcely a word of thanks, the photographers left, to rush their pictures into their papers.

Ben, who had sat to one side during this, now jumped forward, just in time to stop one of the axemen from crashing down on the machine, a beautiful thing that had been plugged into a socket and illuminated for the occasion. Mr. Cantrell looked at him questioningly, but he beckoned the new Chief back to one of the cells in the rear. "Joe, you ever been abroad?"

"No, Ben, I haven't."

"Neither have I, except once to Mexico."

"Mexico, south of the Rio Grande."

"Juarez, across the river from El Paso. Well, when I came back, I thought I'd bring in some perfume. Just a fool notion I had, but—"

"Well, we all get drunk."

"Just what I said to myself. Now get this: On some of that perfume, they got a rule that the customs officer has to destroy the label before it's brought in. You got that?"

"Gee, you sure can spread light, Ben."

"You know how he destroyed it?"

"No, but I'm dying to hear."

"He drew a blue pencil across it. He made one blue mark on it, and legally that destroyed it. Listen, Joe, if one blue mark will destroy a label, why won't it destroy a pinball machine?"

Mr. Cantrell jammed his hands into his trousers pockets and stared at Ben for a long time. "Say, you can think of things, can't you?"

"I do my best."

"You mean, destroy it *legally?*"

"Yeah, legally."

"If you got a blue pencil, I could try."

"I got one, right here."

"Then we'll see."

"And one other thing."

"Yeah, Ben?"

"You'll want those trucks again, hey? To haul the destroyed machines over to the Reservoir Street dump?"

"Why—they got to be put *some* place."

"O.K.—I'll have them here tonight. And if you don't mind, have a police photographer at that dump tomorrow, to take pictures of the destroyed machines. Of course they'll be nothing but junk, but it'll prove I hauled them—and that you destroyed them."

"Funny how a blue pencil ruins stuff, isn't it?"

"Oh, and another thing."

"Just one?"

"Sign these vouchers."

"What vouchers?"

"For the trucks! The trucks I furnished the city yesterday, to haul these gambling machines from various and sundry addresses, here to the Ninth Street station house. Three hundred bucks in all—"

"Hey, what is this?"

"You think trucks work for nothing?"

"No, but I got to check—"

"Costs money to clean a town up, you ought to know that. Now if you'll sign there, where I put the pencil check, I can get over to the hotel with them before they close the safe, and—"

"Won't they keep till tomorrow?"

"Joe, I need cash to pay workmen. I—"

"O.K., Ben, but don't run a good thing to death."

"Nuts, it's the people's will."

"What?"

"You forgot that mandate to cleanliness. Sign."

Around nine, however, Ben wasn't so cynically confident. He walked up and down the main room of a big warehouse with a neat little man in a blue gabardine suit and a soft straw hat. It was a shabby warehouse, and the only illumination was from a single poisonous light hanging very high. He kept looking at his watch, but presently a horn sounded outside, and he hurried to open the big trolley door at one end. Shaking the building, while the man in gabardine yelled to "cut those lights," a truck rolled in, and when it was squarely in the middle of the room, stopped. Cutting lights and motor, three men jumped down, peeled tarpaulins from the load, and proceeded to unload it. It was the same equipment as had been seized, condemned, and legally destroyed in the last twenty-four hours, but appeared to be in quite passable condition. Working rapidly, under the direction of the man in gabardine, the three from the truck stacked the machines against the wall and departed, saying the other crew would report at ten, and from then on they'd make time.

The man in gabardine looked over the machines with

professional interest, testing springs here, counting bright steel balls there. Ben, however, seemed uneasy. Presently he said, "Listen, Mr. Roberts—of course I'm sure you know your business, but are you really sure these games can be transformed?"

"Of course I am."

"Yeah, but—look, this is what I mean. Like in golf, which is one of the games we're going to have, there's only so many things a player can do. He can get in the rough, he can shoot past the green, he can pitch *on* the green, he can sink a putt—I don't know *how* many, but it's just *so* many. Well, suppose that don't correspond to the number of holes on the table? Without we plug some holes up, or put new ones in, or re-design the whole thing, how do we—"

"O.K., now—pick out a table."

"Well, *that* one. What do we make out of it?"

"Baseball."

"*How?*"

"I'll show you."

Taking off his coat, Mr. Roberts went over to a chest that stood in one corner, opened it, and took out a hammer and screw driver, then selected a number of metal clips from little compartments inside that were arranged like printers' type cases. These he dropped into a paper bag. Then he took the table Ben had pointed out, upended it, and screwed legs into it. Then he stood it rightside up, and for a moment inspected its metal fittings, its gleaming pins, springs, and bells. Then he motioned at the legend LUCKY BALL WIN 5¢— 10¢—25¢—$1, which rose over one end. "You understand, that comes off and the new one goes on: Baseball, the National Game, Play One Whole Inning for Five Cents—"

"Yeah, I understand about that part."

"O.K., then. Watch."

Deftly, Mr. Roberts began unscrewing tags that labeled each hole with numbers from 0 to 1,000. Soon Ben interrupted: "All right, I've doped this out. The batter can get a strike, or a ball, or he can single, double, triple, or pole one over the fence, or he can sacrifice, or maybe a couple of other things. Not over fifteen, though. That's top. Well there's exactly twenty holes on that table. What then?"

Without answering, Mr. Roberts began screwing new tags in front of the holes. They bore legends, in neat red letters, of "Strike," "Ball," "Out on Fly," etc., just as Ben had anticipated, but when all of them had been screwed into place there were still four unlabeled holes. Mr. Roberts smiled.

"Now, then, here's where we equalize."

So saying, he screwed on four tags. Ben, peering, saw that two of them read: "Out on foul," and two others, "Hit into Double." On the last two, Mr. Roberts dropped loose metal covers. "Those holes are dead till there's a man on base. Can't have a double play without anybody on. Same way with a sacrifice. But don't you get it? If there's too many holes we equalize by having a few of those holes read the same thing—that doubles the chances for foul balls, maybe, but who says this ain't fast pitching we got? If there's not enough holes, we knock out sacrifice bunt, advance on error, whatever we want. Look: they play the game you got, not the game you wish you had. You get it?"

"Well, gee, it's simple, isn't it?"

"O.K., you be the Gi'nts, I'll be the Dodgers."

"You mean that's all? We can play *now?*"

"I like pinball. Buck on the side?"

"McPhail, show what you got."

"I've singled, big boy."

The midsummer twilight was fading as Ben entered his living room and lit it, not with the wall brackets, which were harsh, but with the floor lamps, which were soft. He checked the contents of a tray which had arrived a few minutes before: shaker, evidently full; two glasses, bottoms up, in a bowl of ice; a saucer of cherries, with fork; a dish of tiny canapes, six anchovies, six eggs, six cheese; two napkins, folded. The buzzer sounded, and he hastened to the door with the springy stride that seemed never to desert him.

June came in, nodded, and sat down, pulling off her gloves. She too had changed since that night a few months ago when she had made the speech at the high school auditorium, and a man had made a note in a little red book. The neat, school-teacherish blue silk had given way to a smart black polka-dot, with belt, bag, and shoes of coral alligator skin, hat of red straw, and stockings of powdery sheer that set off an exciting pair of legs. It all combined beautifully with her dark, creamy good looks, and it seemed that perhaps she knew it. She came in with languid hauteur, or at least the imitation of languid hauteur; it might be recent, but it was innocent.

Ben, however, seemed neither surprised nor unduly upset. He righted the glasses, flipped a cherry in each, and poured the Manhattans. Setting one beside her, he said, "Here's how," took a sip of his own, put it down. Then he took an envelope from the inner pocket of his coat and handed it to her. "Your share."

". . . Of what?"

"Of what we're doing."

"Oh, thanks. I'd forgotten."

"You'd better count it."

She opened the envelope, started in spite of herself when she saw the thick mat of $20's, $10's, and $5's that it contained. Her voice shook a little as she said: "Well—that's very nice."

He suddenly remembered something he had meant to tell her: about a suite that would be vacant next week, at the hotel. It seemed she was living here now, in a suite on the third floor, but the one to be vacated would give her a better view, at the same price. She said something about her apartment, which she had under lease until January 1, and hadn't been able to rent. He made no comment, and she returned to the envelope, actually counting the money this time. Then she counted it again, and drew a trembling breath. Then she lapsed into a long, moody silence. He asked, "How's social service?"

"All right, thank you."

"Plenty of milk for the anemic kids?"

"Not as much as we want, but—"

"That can be fixed. Or helped, anyway."

"Any help will be welcome."

"I told you before, the main kick I get out of having a little dough is to be able to help on a few things where help counts. Tomorrow, I'll send a little check, and it's a promise."

"It'll be quite welcome."

"Speaking of milk, how's Jansen?"

"Very well, the last time I saw him."

"When was that?"

"Does it concern you?"

"Yeah, a little."

". . . It was last night."

"And he was very well, you say?"

"So far as I could see."

"Great work he's doing here. Cleaning the town up—"

"Suppose we leave Mayor Jansen out of this."

"Well—if so, why?"

"This talk about cleaning the town up makes me a little sick to the stomach, I find, especially in view of this dirty money you've handed me."

"What do you mean, dirty?"

"I mean it's gambling money, and from children's gambling, at that. Their nickels and dimes, that they got to buy ice cream with, or earned from their paper routes, or whatever way they got it—about the cleanest money there is, so long as *they* have it. But when we get it, it's dirty, just about the *dirtiest* money there is and I don't want any more talk about the town's being clean."

"Listen, we're operating legitimate enterprises, and—"

"Ben, I know exactly how legitimate our enterprises are, because I patronized one the other day, and stayed with it to the bitter end, to see how it worked. It was a golf game, and it took me an hour to make a hole in one, but finally I did, and received my certificate, with my name written on it in the druggist's flowing script. Then I took it to Room 518 of the Coolidge Building where I had heard that such a certificate can be redeemed for $1. I faced Lefty over a glass-top desk, and he knew who I was and I knew who he was, but we didn't speak. I took the silver dollar he gave me, and went out, and I knew that the legitimacy of our enter-

113

prises is so slight that it probably can't be found by any test known to science. It's dirty money. So let's say no more about it."

"I notice you take it."

"I take it because I happen to have a sister who makes me a great deal of trouble and costs me a great deal of money. I pretend to be romantically interested in a man that's finer, that's worth more, than you and I will ever be, taken together or separately. Because he happens to believe in me he does a great many things that I ask him to do, as Mayor of this city. Because of that, you're able to do things, to operate enterprises, that pay. I take my share, because I have to. I hate it. I hate myself. I hate you, if you must know the truth. And don't let's have any pretense that what we're doing is any different from what it really is."

"How is she, by the way?"

"Who?"

"Your sister. Dorothy."

"She's fine. She's working in a summer camp, it may interest you to know. That money you lent me, that money I had to send the college authorities to cover what she stole, I made up my mind she had to pay it back. I saw to it that she got a job in a summer camp waiting on tables. It's hard work, and she hasn't much time to get into mischief. And she's paying me back. She's paying me back at the rate of $5 a week."

"Aren't you the skinflint."

"There's a principle involved, and she can learn it."

"*Can* anybody learn how to be honest?"

"If not, she can wait on tables in a summer camp."

"That money, by the way, is deducted."

"You mean I get all this in addition to what—to that

two hundred and some that you put up on account of Dorothy?"

"Everything in the envelope is clear."

"My, my."

"—And dirty."

"I—asked you not to talk about that."

"Now suppose you get out."

". . . *What?*"

"We're not going to dinner. You and I are through."

"Oh. I see."

"So beat it."

"Very well, then . . . May I ask *why?*"

"For *you* being dishonest. With *me*."

". . . I still don't—"

"Oh, that's all right. Just go."

She was standing by now, wholly bewildered, every inch the amateur at love who had wooed him so avidly before. He sat on the sofa coldly staring at her. He was suddenly the man who had faced Cantrell. But since then he had faced a great many people, had taken part in countless bullying scenes. It was impossible to tell where reality began in him, and where play-acting ended; everything, in a sense, had become a colossal bluff, and apparently something of the sort figured here. He watched her as she started for the door, made no sign as she stopped and came marching back, her bottom switching quickly, angrily, absurdly. "So you're throwing me out, is that it?"

"Yes."

"That's what you think. Mr. Benjamin Grace, you have just about three seconds to take back what you've said to me and apologize for it. If you don't, I'm going straight to Mr. Jansen, who, as you probably know, is

Mayor of this town. I'm going to tell him everything you've done, everything you're doing, and there, I think, will go your perfectly legitimate enterprises, and the thousands you hope to make out of them, and——"

"Get out."

Her mouth twitched as her little flurry crumpled, and once more she started for the door. This time when she stopped and turned, tears were running down her cheeks, and she was cravenly contrite. "Ben, what have I done? Why are you doing this to me?"

"That's more like it. Keep on talking."

"I don't understand——"

"Keep talking!"

"What—do you want me to say?"

He got up, yanked off her hat, sent it skimming into a chair. He cuffed the back of her head so her hair went tumbling over her face. With a quick hip movement, reminiscent of football, he sent her spinning to the sofa. Then he stood over her. "Get this: you can go to Jansen any time you want. If you want to go now, you can go now, and I'll help you out that door with a kick."

"Ben, I don't understand you. I——"

"Then I'll make it plain. In the first place, don't try to tell me you're hooked up with me on account of that bum, Dorothy. She's all paid up, and you've got a grand in that envelope, and so far as she's concerned you got no obligation whatever. You know why you're doing it?"

"It's Dorothy! I've told you, she's been——"

"It's not Dorothy. You know who it is?"

". . . Yes."

"Then who is it?"

"You."

"That's right."

116

He stood away from her, lit a cigarette, while she broke down and cried, great tears squirting out of her eyes and streaming down her face. "That's right, it's me. And from now on suppose you don't forget it."

"I've heard of men like you."

"What do you mean, men like me?"

"Men that pretend to love a girl, and then make her go out and—love other men for the money they bring back, and—"

"Are you loving Jansen?"

"Almost."

"That word is important."

"I don't see that it is."

"It is to me."

"Ben, why do you treat me like this?"

"Didn't you hear me? If you want to go, you can."

"I don't want to. I can't."

"Now we got that straight at last."

He sat at the other end of the sofa, squashed his cigarette, looked at her with heavy-lidded eyes, said, "Now we can talk about love." She had doubled over into a tiny knot, her face on her knees, and there ensued an interval in which she sobbed, and twisted her handkerchief, and seemed to go through some sort of inner struggle. Then she threw herself on him, held her mouth against his, twisted his hair with her fingers, and gave way to tremulous, half-sobbing little laughs.

8

Lefty, dropping in at Ben's apartment, looked exactly as he had looked the day of the Castleton robbery; the elegant surroundings, indeed, only accentuated his ill-fitting suit, his bandy-legged walk, his air of bucolic simplicity. He came in with a friendly hello, marched vacantly around for a few moments, then stood at the window, taking in the view from the high tower of the hotel. The whole city was visible, and in the distance the lake looked blue under the haze of approaching autumn. Something caught his ear. He looked, and a smile spread over his face. "Did you hear it, Ben? There's nothing like it, I swear there isn't—that sound of a shoe on a football. I knew it, soon as I heard it, and sure enough, there they are down there, kicking it around. Don't you love it?"

"Not noticeably."

Surprised, Lefty turned around. Ben seemed dejected. He sat on the sofa, his elbows on his knees, and stared at his feet. They were turned inwards, with a juvenile, ineffectual, pigeon-toed effect that enhanced the suggestion of smallness that hung over everything that he did. Lefty blinked, then laughed. "Oh—I forgot."

"You expect me to love football you'll be disappointed."

"How long did you play, Ben?"

"I played grammar school, my last two years, then four years high school. I played three years college, then two more years college, under a phony name, until a place up the line found out who I was and I had to quit. Then I played two years pro. I played so many games I can't remember them all, and them that I can remember, I generally don't if I can help it."

"Thirteen years, altogether."

"Something like that."

"What position did you play?"

"I started in the line, because I was big. When I was sixteen I weighed one seventy. I played guard and tackle, and my last year high school I played center. Then my growth caught up and I began to get fast and they moved me out to end. Then they found out I could pass and for a season I played quarter, but I was no good at it."

"Why not?"

"Dumb on plays."

"Where next?"

"Two steps rear. Somewhere along the line I'd learned to kick, and I did all right at fullback. Then I began to show class at broken-field running, and they shifted me to half. That was what I was really good at, staying with an interference and holding my feet in a field. I was good for a couple of yards even after I was tackled—just stagger yardage, but it helped. Sometimes you could score with it. At that stuff I was O.K."

"Every position there was, hey?"

"Oh, and coach, I forgot. My last year at pro."

"And still you don't like it?"

"You ever play, Lefty?"

"Little bit in high school."

"I never saw a player that liked it. Maybe he tells the girls he likes it but he wouldn't try to tell another player and get away with it. There's nothing about it to like. First you got to train. You can't take punishment and smoke, booze, or do any of those things. Then it hurts. All of it hurts, from blocking an end to blocking a punt. Boy, is that one for the books, taking a football right in the puss and then grabbing it to score. And there's no soft spots, like in baseball where you play half the game on the bench. It's all right, I guess. You get some cheers and you get some dough. But the cheers, they're in the stand and the dough's in the dressing room. What goes on out there on the field is just nothing to write home about. I hear those kids down there, kicking it around, sure I hear them. But I'm not getting up to look. You don't mind, do you?"

"Say, that's a laugh."

"What's a laugh?"

"You, dumb on plays. You can call 'em now, hey?"

"They said I was dumb, and I let it go at that, but that wasn't really my trouble. When a guy was all in, when he was out on his feet and had no more to give, I hated to hit him with the whip. I kept trying to do it myself. Well, there's spots in a game where a quarterback run's not smart, that's all. I got the same trouble now. I call 'em, because I got to. But I don't like it any, and

I'm always wishing I could do it myself. What's on your mind?"

"Cantrell."

"And what about him?"

"He wants to see you."

"I'm right here and I'm not made of glass."

"Ben, can I say something?"

"Sure, go ahead."

"Why can't you be like you used to be, a guy that was reasonable and that somebody could get along with? What are you trying to pull off, anyhow? A bum imitation of Solly Caspar? It's not you, Ben. For instance, there's no reason why you can't drop over to see Cantrell. And you ought to. Chief of Police is no office boy's job. And he's dangerous. He can do things to you."

"You really want to know?"

"I do, indeed. We're pals, aren't we?"

"I got to make him come here."

"Why?"

"Well, in the first place I tried being nice to Joe. I tried being reasonable and doing business the way I like to do it. And what happened? He began telling me where to get off. He began measuring it up, what he'd take and what he wouldn't take. And right there was when I remembered something I'd been trying to forget—something you said that day when we were fanning along waiting for the bank to be held up. You said: A big operator, he runs it or he don't operate. And what I was trying to be was a big operator. It was just a piece of luck that gave me the chance, but there it was, if I wanted it. You think I was letting Cantrell stand in my way? You think I was caring about his feelings? I let him have it. I *got* to make him come here. If I don't

I got no team. Call him up now. Tell him to come over."

"Look, you call him. I—"

"Didn't you hear me? I said call him."

Mr. Cantrell, who always looked as though he had just emerged from a barber shop, arrived in a surprisingly short time. He said that by a singular coincidence he was on his way to this very hotel, on another matter, when Lefty caught him. He asked how do you explain that? He said his wife was a great believer in thought transference, but that he himself didn't pay much attention to it, except that when something like this happens it sure does look funny. He said Ben was gaining weight, the least little bit. He said: "What's bothering you, Ben?"

"Heard you wanted to see me."

"Yeah, there's a couple of things."

"Uncouple them, then."

"Like, for instance, the bookies."

"They giving trouble?"

"Well, have we got bookies, or not?"

"Well, they're there, aren't they?"

"Yeah, but are they *supposed* to be there?"

"Go on, Joe. What's the rest of it?"

"Well, look, this Jansen has tasted glory and he likes it, see? After I cleaned up pinball and he got all those editorials in the newspapers patting him on the back, why, he wants more, only a lot. Well, there they are, those bookies, and there's Jansen, coming in to my office every day, talking about them."

"Does Jansen really buy it, what we did on pinball?"

"He's fooled, right down the line."

"He thinks pinball is cleaned up?"

"Listen, on stuff like that, Jansen's not any too bright. You remember, even in the campaign he wasn't getting anywhere till that girl got in it—this Lyons that he's put in charge of the Social Service department. Maybe she could tell him about pinball, but she don't seem to be doing it, for some reason. Maybe the police department could tell him, but I don't regard that as advisable just now. Maybe the District Attorney could tell him, but his law firm is working for you, the last I heard of it. So nobody's telling him. So he thinks he's done a big job. Well, is he so dumb? Didn't every paper in town eat it up, us grabbing those machines, and destroying them? Has any one of them taken the trouble to investigate these new machines, and find out who owns them, or how they work?"

"And Jansen's hot after the bookies now?"

"I don't talk about the neighborhood places. He don't know so much about them. But these big dumps downtown, if he keeps on, I'll have to close them down. Well, what about it? You're supposed to know, and you're not telling me."

"You seen Delany?"

". . . Haven't *you* seen him?"

"I've been letting those bookies alone."

"Ben, you don't mean you haven't *collected* off them?"

"What else you got?"

"The houses."

"What houses?"

"The ones with red lights in front."

"And what about them?"

"The same, only worse. In addition to Jansen, I got

the men on the beat to worry about. I mean, they've begun taking it off those places direct, and that's bad. It leaves everything wide open for a stink any time the grand jury happens to stumble on it. The way Caspar did, he collected that dough and made the kick-back himself, so there was nobody that had anything on the cops direct. This way it's just a mess with anything likely to pop. I don't even dare bust a sergeant for fear he'll crack it open."

"What else?"

"Paroles."

"And what about *them?*"

"You know what about them. They bought their paroles, a whole slew of these mugs. They bought them off Caspar, and he made the kick-back, so the police would let them alone. Only a lot of them couldn't pay it all at once and they still owe the dough on the deals that were made before they got sprung. Well, now Caspar has skipped. Have you collected any of that money?"

"No."

"You going to?"

"I'll let you know."

"I want to know now."

They had been sitting, or at least Lefty and Mr. Cantrell had been sitting, near the low cocktail table that stood in front of Ben's fireplace, Lefty in a big armchair, Mr. Cantrell on the sofa. Ben, a little restless, had walked aimlessly about, smoking into two or three ashtrays, listening to Mr. Cantrell intently, if without any evidence of enjoyment. At the rasp in Mr. Cantrell's voice his head came slowly around and his big, lithe body stiffened. Mr. Cantrell met his gaze for a long second, then looked away. ". . . Or pretty soon, anyway."

"I thought that's what you meant."

"Well, look, Ben, there's no argument about it, we got a nice set-up if we can just hold our lead. But we can't sit around and let things slide. I got to know where I'm at, the bookies have got to know, my men have got to know. *I got to know who's running this.* If it's you— O.K., you know how to run it, or ought to, by now. But if you're not *going* to run it, why—"

"I'll let you know."

After Mr. Cantrell had gone, Ben resumed his restless walk, then went into the pantribar, poured two glasses of beer, came out, set one in front of Lefty. His own he sipped standing up, blotting the foam from his lips with his handkerchief. "You heard what he said, Lefty?"

"Well, somebody's got to collect that money."

"That's what *he* thinks."

"Well?"

"You think I can treat him decent?"

"You can be reasonable."

"Not with him I can't, or with you, or with any of you. He wants his dough, and that's all he wants. If he don't get it—say, is Goose Groner around?"

"I haven't seen him. Why?"

"I think I need a guard."

"Bugs Lenhardt's in town."

"I don't want Bugs. I could use Goose, though. . . . Do I look like a guy that would take it off women? Dumb girls that haven't any more sense, or that maybe ran into some tough luck and got started on something they couldn't stop? Or off parolees? Poor cons that are trying to get a fresh start, and only ask that the cops let them alone."

"I told you already. Someone's going to take it."

"Would *you* take it?"

"Nobody's asking me to."

"Being a big operator, it's not all gravy."

"Pretty near all."

"No, pal, no."

Ben looked a little surprised when the clerk asked him to have a seat, and said Mr. Delany would be right down. The main lobby of the Lakeside Country Club, with men, women, and children scampering about, did seem like an odd sort of place to discuss a confidential matter of bookmaking. However, if that was the way Mr. Delany chose to do business, there wasn't much help for it, so Ben sat down, lit a cigarette, and watched the animated scene at rear, where four pretty girls prepared to tee off the terrace that inaugurated the pleasant rolling golf course.

Before he could get up, a tall thin man dropped into the chair across the table from him, nodded briefly, and contemplated him with a hostile, lowering stare. It was not the first time Ben had seen Mr. Delany, but it was the first time he had met him, and he looked at him with considerable interest. He was, indeed, a curious type, as American in appearance as a streamlined hearse, as world-wide in distribution as the gambling on which he lived. He was an adventurer, and illustrated a frequently-forgotten principle: If a man but worship the great god horse, he may associate with whom he pleases, and few will inquire as to his morals, his honor, or his means of support. Mr. Delany chose to associate with the outdoor set of Lake City, where he was born, and since he was unmarried, to live at the Lakeside Club. He came of passable family, but gossip had it that his early life had been hard, and that he had improved his circumstances by paying attention to influential ladies, who had gained him entree into certain clubs. Then he had played polo. As he was even taller than Ben, who was over six feet, and thin, and a fine rider, he cut a figure at this, and acquired a rating. Then he bought horses and became a gentleman jockey. Then he began an association with bookmakers, though he promulgated the fiction that this was an amusing outgrowth of his equine activities, a matter of no importance. His associations developed into what are known as connections, particularly in Chicago, and eventually with Mr. Caspar. Now, at the age of forty, he was a lean, leathery man, who faced Ben in breeches, boots, and rough tweed coat, and spoke with a cavalryman's voice: curt, clipped, and harsh, but with a touch of the grand manner.

After the moment in which he eyed Ben as sharply as Ben eyed him, he began with no word of greeting: "All right, Grace, what did you come here about?"

"I thought I told you over the phone: Business."

"Then state it."

"Some bookies are operating downtown. You and Caspar ran those boys, I believe—you because you had a hook-up with Chicago, and he because he was Mr. Big around town here, and between the two of you it was a pretty good set-up. Well, Caspar's not here any more now, and to some extent I've taken things over. The matter I wanted to take up with you is whether you'd like to come in with me, running those bookies, and we'd do it on pretty much the same arrangement as you had with Caspar."

"No."

"It would be unfortunate if those bookies got closed."

"The answer is still no."

"May I ask why?"

"You killed my brother."

For the first time Ben realized that the eyes that glowered across the table at him held hate, not merely ill-humor. He licked his lips, blinked, heard himself say: "I—I didn't kill your brother."

"Not alone. Caspar instigated it, if that's what you mean. But you were in it. You were one of those rats and you helped dispose of his body."

"Wait a minute, Mr. Delany. I was not in on it. I drove Caspar the night it was done, and I knew something was afoot. But that often happened with Sol, as you may imagine, and I give you my word I knew nothing about your brother until two days later, when they lifted him out of Koquabit Narrows. I thought it was Arch Rossi they had got, if you have to know what I thought. And you may be interested to know that it was I, working with Miss Lyons, who made the discovery of that body. You didn't know that, did you?"

"Yes."

"Then—"

"I knew it, and I think you played it both ways. I think you helped kill my brother, and then I think you crossed Caspar, and showed June Lyons where the body was. Now get this, Grace. I didn't want to see you at all. But for the last week you've been calling me and sending me messages, and I thought it best to settle this with you, once and for all. In the first place if I see you again, I'm going to kill you, and I advise you to stay out of my way. In the second place, I decided to see you today in a public place, where there'd be twenty witnesses to what happened, if anything. I'm unarmed, and I have three men, within twenty feet of me as I sit here, who'll grab me if I start anything. But get this: if you don't keep out of my way you're playing with death, and nothing can save you. Now get out."

The muscles in Mr. Delany's brown, leathery cheeks began to work, and his hands gripped the arms of his chair. Ben, his eyes flickering, got up, turned, started for the door. He walked with unhurried calm, and yet his heels seemed to lift a little, just a little too quickly as he neared the door. A man, sitting near a pillar with a golf club in his hand, watched him with a fish-faced stare.

Once more the sirens were screeching in Lake City, and this time they led the trucks to the six bookmaking establishments that Ben had visited the day he first saw June. Once more equipment was carted off: blackboards, with certain electrical attachments, and many boxes of tickets, with stub-books. And once more there was a hearing in Mr. Himmelhaber's court, with heavy fines being levied this time, and once more there were photographers at the old Ninth Street station house, taking pictures of equipment being destroyed in accordance with court orders. But on this occasion Ben wasn't present, and the next day actual fires were visible on the Reservoir Street dump.

About a week later, on Market Street, near the center of town, a place opened for business. It was a regulation store front, but lettered on the window was the legend:

Above was the trademark of the firm, a winged Mercury holding lightly to the tailskid of an airplane, and below was a group of horses, running under a blanket, their jockeys swinging whips. Quite a crowd gathered the day of the opening, and to these Ben made a little speech, or rather a series of speeches, for he kept saying the same thing over and over, in a sort of mechanical sing-song:

"This is a messenger service, not a bookmaking establishment. We don't post odds, and for information about horses, jockeys, or track conditions you will have to consult the daily papers which are posted on the board at right. If you wish us to do so, we shall transmit any money you give us to S. Cartogensis & Son at Castleton, in a sealed envelope, whose perforated stub you will retain. Any instructions for use of the money you can place inside the envelope using the printed cards on the table at my left if you like. Any remittances to you from Cartogensis we shall be glad to transmit, and the perforated stub which you retain will be sufficient evidence of identity. The charge will be two and one half percent—five cents for every two-dollar remittance which we accept. The plane will leave every hour on the hour—first at noon, in time for the placing of remittances on horses running on Eastern tracks, then every hour thereafter until four, when the final trip will be flown. This is a messenger service, not a bookmaking establishment . . ."

The sirens led the way to this place, too, and quickly, for they arrived the very afternoon it opened, and Ben was ceremoniously driven to headquarters in the newest and shiniest patrol truck. Mr. Cantrell was worried as they sat in the captain's office, just before they started for Magistrate Himmelhaber's court. "This is no way to do, Ben. If you had to do it, if there was no way to get out of the pinch, then O.K. But nobody but a cluck would go out of his way to get pulled on a thing like this."

"You ever been to Washington, Joe?"

"Once, when I was married."

"Did you hock something?"

"No, we bought round-trip tickets."

"I don't know how it is now, but hock shops used to be illegal in the District of Columbia. The government clerks, they were in hock so bad that something had to be done about it, so hock shops were made against the law. You know how they got around that?"

"Messenger service?"

"That's right. There was a place just off the avenue that had a motorcycle service. It ran over to Virginia, and you gave them your watch, and they ran it over there for you, and one hour later you came back and got your money."

"But that was—different."

"I don't see any difference."

Whether Mr. Cantrell's face was any redder than usual, whether his expression of embarrassment was real or feigned, it would be hard to say. At any rate, he received a stiff reprimand in court. Mr. Bleeker, the District Attorney, was no more unpleasant about it than he could help, but he made it plain that if the police, instead of taking things in their own hands, had consulted his office about it, the town would be spared an exhibition of over-zealousness that went beyond anything in his experience. The truth was, he went on without bothering to look at his former partner, Mr. Yates, who was defending Ben, that there was no law under which the case could be prosecuted. So long as no book was made in Lake City, so long as the Mercury Company acted solely to transmit moneys entrusted to their care, there was nothing that could be done about it and he would have to move to dismiss. Mr. Himmelhaber nodded. "Chief Cantrell, this doesn't happen to be your case."

"I acted as I thought best, your honor."

"As Castleton is across the state line, it's clearly a Federal matter, so I wholly agree with Mr. Bleeker: there's nothing for me to do but dismiss your prisoner."

"It's not up to me to decide it, your honor."

"This is a Federal matter."

Mr. Yates soliloquized a little, as soon as he and Ben were on the street again. "You'd think it was a Federal matter. It would certainly *seem* that they'd have a law covering it, so the F.B.I., or somebody, could take charge and rub you out. However, they haven't. I've been looking it up. It's perfectly legal."

The five o'clock Mercury plane was just winging in as Ben poured June's cocktail, and he stepped to the window to admire it. "Look at that little green beauty—and think what she's bringing in with her. All but one favorite lost today, and that means there'll be four hundred we split on this one trip alone. Plenty of dough you're making for Dorothy. How is she, by the way?"

"She's all right, thank you."

"Summer camp closed?"

"Yes. I sent her back to college."

"Oh—I didn't know that."

"Not to the one she'd been attending, of course. I

couldn't have got her back there, after the trouble over the—missing articles. But there's another little place where they accepted her, and she can complete her senior year."

"Near here?"

"Does it matter?"

"Just being sociable."

"I prefer not to say."

The plane was dipping down for the airport now and Ben watched it for a minute or two, taking sips out of his cocktail, always blotting his lips with his handkerchief.

Presently he said: "I love that little thing. And the beauty of it is, the whole thing's on the up-and-up. We're not putting anything over on Jansen this time. It's legal, the District Attorney says it's legal, the court says it's legal. And to think of what Delany would have cut in for, if he'd wanted to stick—just because he knows a lug in Chicago by the name of Frankie Horizon. The hook-up in Castleton was so easy it made me laugh. The cops fixed it up on account of the favor we did them after the bank stick-up. You and I, we just didn't realize that we'd made a few pretty good friends."

"Do you have to say 'we'?"

"Anything you like."

"I'd rather you left me out, if you don't mind."

Ben sighed, went around turning on the lights, took June's coat from her, hung it in a closet. It was a mink coat, of smart length and cut, and he admired it before he slipped it on the hanger. At any rate he sank his nose into it, to feel its softness, and to smell it. He seemed to be in an amiable humor. He sat on the arm of her chair, touched her black curls.

"One thing I did I think you'll like."

"What's that?"

"I ended this parole racket."

"How do you mean?"

"Quite a few of them owed money for paroles they'd bought—to Caspar, I mean. I could have made them cough up, if I'd wanted to. In fact, Cantrell was after me to turn on the heat. Nice guy, Cantrell is. . . . I told him it was out. If those people got out of jail, it's O.K. by me and they got nothing to fear from me. From now on they can start their lives over again, and I wish them all the luck in the world. You got anything against it?"

"Why should I?"

Her tone, which was wholly indifferent, rebuffed him. In a moment he said, "One other thing I did I *know* you're going to like."

"Yes? What's that?"

"Those houses. The red light places. I'm closing them down. I told Cantrell there was a few things I'd stop at, and one of them was taking it off a lot of poor girls for leading a life of—"

He stopped at the sudden blaze in her eyes. "But you'd take it off me, wouldn't you?"

"What do you mean, take it off you?"

"For leading a life of shame with Jansen, for doing just what those girls do, for keeping him under my thumb, so you can fool him with airplanes flying around, and pinball games that pretend to be something that they're not—for these little services, you're perfectly willing that I lead a life of shame, aren't you?"

"Are you that close to Jansen?"

"No, but if I had to be, you'd be perfectly willing. If

134

it was a choice between my honor and the money, you'd rather have the money, wouldn't you?"

His face darkened and he lit a cigarette. Then he began the restless marching around that seemed to be his main occupation these days. After a few minutes he stopped in front of her, gave her foot an affectionate little kick. "What's the use of having one of these every week, anyhow? You know I don't want you to do anything with Jansen. You know that, because I've told you so—"

"Ben, keep quiet or I'll scream!"

Ben filled both glasses, emptied ashtrays, did as many little things as he could think of, then at length sat down. She had been staring at the ceiling, and now began to talk in a dull, lifeless way. "His wife died today."

"Whose?"

"Jansen's."

"When?"

"Just now. Before I came over here."

"I—haven't seen the papers."

"He asked me to step down to his office, as he had something to tell me. I went down there, and this was it. He was terribly broken up about it. I did what I could to help him. Then—he asked me to marry him. He hadn't intended to, then. He was going to wait till after the funeral. But it was the first time I had kissed him, and he broke down, and said it. And I said I would. And that was what I came over to tell you—"

"Hey, wait, this affects me."

"Oh, don't worry. That was optimism, over there in his office. I'll not marry him. How could I, after what I've done to him? After what you and I have done to him? After all that he'd find out about me, that a hundred people would tell him, if I were ever fool enough to do this to him?"

Apparently there was more, but she couldn't go on. She broke down into low, hopeless sobbing, which went on for some time. Then she jumped up and threw her glass at him.

9

Emerging from the bathroom in white shorts, Ben started the immemorial rite of donning a white tie, while Lefty lounged in the bedroom armchair, a fascinated witness. It was not, on the whole, an uninteresting performance, as Ben went through with it. For one thing there was Ben himself, as he stooped over the bed, putting studs into the shirt, checking collar, tie, and socks. Great muscles rippled in his torso, in his arms, in his shoulders, then disappeared. There was that curious accuracy of movement that seemed to mark everything he did: the sure way his fingers managed tiny problems, like buttonholes; the instinctive order that he achieved, so that nothing seemed to get lost. And then there was the absurdly brief investiture itself, the actual putting of the garments on. This show seemed to be all preparation, for once the harness was ready, it went on in a few seconds, even to tying the tie. Lefty missed no single detail, and even admitted he would give anything to be able to wear such an outfit. When he looked at his watch he started. "You going to a show you better shake a foot. It's after nine o'clock already."

"Show? This is a party."

"Oh—must be some shindig."

"June's giving it."

"You still see her?"

"Now and then, mostly then. Her old lady crossed her up on Christmas. 'Stead of having her and her sister home, she decided she and the sister would visit June. So they came, and June had to throw them a party."

"You heard anything about her and Jansen?"

"No, I haven't."

"They say they're thick."

"Who says?"

"It's going around."

"You couldn't prove it by me."

For a moment Lefty had watched Ben narrowly, but if the inquiry meant anything to him, Ben gave no sign. He led the way into the living room, got out Scotch, ice, and soda, and turned on the radio. Dance music came in.

"You know one thing, Lefty? The best thing about the night after Christmas is you don't have to listen to those hymns any more."

"I don't know. I kind of like them."

"I don't mind them, except for one thing. There's not over five or six of them and they sing them over and over again. After 'Come All Ye Faithful' and 'Silent Night, Holy Night' and 'It Came Upon a Midnight Clear,' why then, what have you got?"

"Trouble with you is, you just don't like music."

"Come to think of it, maybe that's right."

"I know all them hymns."

"Words and all?"

"I ever tell you how I started, Ben?"

"In a reform school, wasn't it?"

"In a way it was. They put me in a reform school, and I wore a denim suit, and worked on the farm, setting out tomato plants, and hoeing onions, and thinning corn. Corn was the worst. It almost broke your back. Then I got reformed. I got religion, and when they let me out I went around preaching. And then one summer I hooked up with a big evangelist, him doing the big night meeting and me talking to the young people in the afternoon. And the night of the big thank offering, I got all the dough, at the point of a gun from the treasurer of the outfit with a handkerchief over my face. But he caught my walk, as I skipped around the corner. He knew me by that, and they got me. That's how I know all them hymns, Ben. I started out as a preacher."

Even Ben, a little too prone to accept everything in life as an everyday occurrence, blinked at this recital. Lefty got out his wallet and began thumbing through the wad of papers it contained. He found what he wanted, a tattered square which he handled carefully, so as not to tear it. Handing it to Ben, he said, "A regular preacher with a license." Ben read the printing, under the imprimatur of some obscure sect, glanced at the signature, which was written over the title, Bishop of Missoula, Montana, and stared at the name which had been typed into the body of the certificate: Richard Hosea Gauss. He handed it back. "Well, say, I never knew that. That's a funny one, isn't it? I bet you could make them holler amen, too."

"I still can."

". . . Little highball?"

"You notice I generally drink beer?"

"Hold everything."

Ben disappeared into the pantribar, came back with two tall glasses, collaring creamily within a perilously short distance of the tops. He set one in front of Lefty, apologizing for being forgetful. Lefty took a meditative sip, waiting for the little *hic* that would follow. When it came, he said, "I guess maybe it's a hangover from them revival days, but it always seemed to me that liquor was wrong. However—there can't be no harm in beer."

"Remember Pearl Harbor."

"Oh we wouldn't forget that."

The party that Ben descended to, in Drawing Room B, was typically citified. That is to say, the clothes, the food, and the service were streamlined, straight out of the Twenty-First Century; the manners, the flirtation, the wit, a little dull. June had invited the whole Social Service Bureau, which was mainly feminine, and these ladies had brought husbands, lovers, and friends who ran a little to spectacles; she had invited also the firm of lawyers for whom she had worked before she entered politics, and these gentlemen had brought their wives; she had invited the city comptroller, the city assessor, the city engineer, and various other officials with whom she came in daily contact, and these gentlemen had not only brought their wives, but in some cases their whole families, consisting of in-laws, daughters, and sons. A few of the gentlemen wore white ties, but most of them wore black, and one or two of them red; there were even a few uniforms present; the party certainly didn't lack for variety. Nor did it lack for spirit.

The Looney Lolligaggers, a five-piece orchestra that the hotel recommended for small private parties, was dispensing its tunes, and most of the guests were dancing. The lunacy of the Lolligaggers, so far as one could see, consisted mainly of bouncing up and down as they blew into their instruments; otherwise they seemed to be very usual boys in white mess jackets.

June let Ben in with civility rather than hospitality. She wore a bottle green dress, with bracelet, comb, and cigarette holder of the coral that she seemed so fond of. Now that the schoolteacherishness had been somewhat dissolved in cocktails, tears, and a conviction of sin, she was really a striking-looking woman, and it didn't hurt the general effect that she was mainly ankles and eyes. Uneasily she took a look at the dancers, said she guessed he knew everyone there. By this he knew that she didn't want to introduce him around. He nodded coolly, said he certainly knew everyone he wanted to know. She said drinks were being served in the alcove, that the waiters would take care of him. He said thanks, and started to edge his way around the floor.

His path was blocked, almost at once, by a dumpy little woman in light blue, who looked first at him and then at June in a timid, uncertain way. June hesitated, then said, "Oh, this is my mother. Mamma, Mr. Grace."

"I'm very glad to know you, Mrs. Lyons."

"What was the name?"

"Grace, but just call me Ben."

"I don't hear very well. I thought at first she said Jansen. I'm just crazy to meet him. I hear he's such a wonderful man."

"Mamma, I told you he's not coming."

"I said, I didn't *rightfully hear.*"

"Mrs. Lyons, a drink?"

"Yes, thanks."

Again Ben started past the dancers, this time guiding Mrs. Lyons by the arm, and again his way was blocked, by a slender, willowy girl with light hair in a peach-colored evening dress. She glanced with a smile at Mrs. Lyons, stepped lightly aside. Mrs. Lyons said, "And this is my other daughter. Dorothy, I want you to meet Mr. Grace, Mr. Ben—"

But Dorothy was gone, slipping between dancers with quick, sure ease, never once getting bumped. Ben, the former broken-field runner, watched fascinated. However, his brow puckered with puzzlement as he turned back to the mother, for he was sure Dorothy had heard.

Mrs. Lyons, once he camped down with her near the potted plants that flanked the alcove, turned out to be more of a trial than he had bargained for. For one thing, she was slightly deaf. For another thing, she was a little tight. For still another thing, she seemed to be under the impression that she was attending a function of high society, and to be elaborately nervous as to the niceties of her conduct. He tried to get her talking about June, of whom she seemed very proud, but she kept returning to the subject, titivating her imagination by wondering if she was properly dressed, if she was downing her drink in an elegant manner, if she should find dancing partners for a stag line that seemed to be forming near the punch bowl. First by one trick, then another trick, he managed to keep her under control. June seemed appreciative, for her frostiness eased a little, and she came over now and then, stood beside him, caught his hand, and squeezed it.

It was when she was drifting away, after one of these visits, that she stopped stock still and stared. The buzzer had sounded, a waiter had opened the door, and Mayor Jansen was entering the room.

There was a murmur, then the Looney Lolligaggers broke off their tune and launched into "O Sapphire Gem of Glory," the Lake City municipal anthem. Mr. Jansen smiled, bowed, and allowed his hat and coat to be taken from him. He had not put on evening clothes, no doubt because his dark gray suit gave suitable emphasis to the mourning band that was sewed prominently on his sleeve. Otherwise he had changed, in ways too subtle for the naked eye, from the archetype of a Swedish dairyman into the archetype of an American Mayor. He was handsome, oily, and absurd. He had a word, a bow, and a smirk for everybody. When the anthem finished, he shook hands with June, then with her at his elbow made the circuit of the room.

When he got to Ben, he said: "Hello, please to meet you, nice party June geev us, hey, yes?" But when he got to Mrs. Lyons, he bowed low, kissed her hand, and said: "Ah, Mamma, Mamma, I been looking forwert dees meeting so much."

He said quite a little more, and she interrupted with little answers, trying to get started, but before she could do so June had him by the elbow again, leading him away, introducing him to people on the other side of the palms. Mrs. Lyons watched hungrily, then caught the expression "Mr. Mayor," as somebody bellowed it from the alcove. Horror-stricken, she turned to Ben. "Is that what you call him? Oh, I called him Mayor. I—"

"It's O.K. Anything."

"But I've got to apologize—"

"He's getting paid for it! What difference does it make? It's a free country, go up and call him Olaf and he's got to take it."

"Call him Olaf—why?"

"It's his name."

She settled back, shedding boozy tears and watching while His Honor passed a group of men, then happily squared off to face six women, all of them young, all of them reasonably pretty. Suddenly she wriggled in her chair, making ready to get up. "Hey, where you going?"

"There's something I completely forgot."

"Yeah, and what's that?"

"Mr. Grace, I have to congratulate him."

"Oh, he got elected six months ago."

"No, no, I mean on his engagement. To June."

"His—where did you hear that?"

"Oh, she didn't tell me. She wouldn't give me the satisfaction. She thinks I'm dumb, she always treats me as if I didn't have good sense. His secretary told me. She was over here, the day before Christmas, bringing the flowers he sent, and—she told me. Let go of me. I've got to congratulate him. I—"

Ben, however, didn't let go of her. He held her firmly by the wrist until she subsided into another trickle of tears. Then he wig-wagged June. Busy with her important guest, she looked away. The next time he caught her eye his face was a thundercloud and in a moment she came over. "June, which is her deaf ear?"

"She can't hear you now. What is it?"

"You better get her out of here."

"What's the trouble?"

"She wants to congratulate him. On the engagement."

"What are you doing, being funny?"

"If so, why?"

"How would she know about—the engagement?"

"His secretary, darling."

June's eyes dilated until they seemed like big black pools, then she took her mother by the arm. Mrs. Lyons was quite amiable about it, and permitted herself to be led, as long as she was under the impression that she was being taken over to Mr. Jansen. When she saw she was headed for the door, however, she began to balk, and June had a ticklish time. Guests turned their backs, so as not to see the pathetic figure in blue, gesticulating foolishly toward the Mayor, and the Looney Lolligaggers suddenly started the "Maine Stein Song." This was played through, however, before June got Mrs. Lyons through the door.

Ben lit a cigarette of relief, and smoked for a few moments alone. Then he became aware of the figure that was standing on the other side of the palms. Dorothy, in her peach-colored dress, stared out at the room. It was the first time he had really had a look at this girl who had started such a chain of circumstances in his life, and he looked with lively interest. It was all the more lively, since he was totally unable to connect this face with all he knew about its owner. It was, in anybody's contest, an extremely beautiful face. It was perfectly chiseled, in profile, at least, its slightly droopy lines reminding him of pictures he had seen of ancient sculpture. There was some exquisite invitation about the mouth: it pursed a little, with an expression of expectancy. The skin was soft, with just a brush of bloom on it. What he could see of the figure was lovely too, not too tall, but slender, soft, willowy. He had decided

145

that there must be some mistake when their glances met, and he saw the kleptomaniac.

Her eye had a bright, dancing light in it.

He squashed his cigarette, looked at the palms of his hands. They had pips of moisture on them. He had the dizzy, half-nauseated feeling of a man who has been rocked to the depths by a woman, and knows it. He got up, crossed in front of her, went into the alcove for a drink. When he had downed a hooker of rye he looked and she was still there. He started to cross in front of her again, and instead stood looking at her. He was to one side of her, and a little behind, only a few inches away. Soon he knew that she knew he was there. After a bellowing silence he heard himself say: "You're bad."

"I didn't speak to you."

"I said you're bad."

"Leave me alone. You belong to her."

"Says who?"

"I heard her call up everybody, to invite them here. When she came to you, I knew you were hers. Why do you talk to me? I haven't said a thing to you."

She leaned against the wall. Her head tilted up and she closed her eyes. His heart was pounding now. He knew he was courting danger, knew he should drift away, and all he could do about it was begin to talk rapidly, so he could finish before June got back: "You can break away from this party. You can if you want to. I'm going to break away. And I'll be on the sixteenth floor, in Number sixteen twenty-eight. You go up in the elevator, that's all. You slip away from the party and go right up in the elevator. You don't even need a coat."

Her eyes opened. She stared straight ahead of her,

and for a long time she said nothing. Then she licked her lips. "You're bad, too."

"We're both bad."

Through the stillness of early morning, so profound that even the faint whine of elevator cables was audible, came the sound of hammering fists: a woman in green, with a great coral comb in her hair, was beating on the door of 1628. She took off one slipper, beat with the heel of that. Across the hall, a door opened and a middle-aged man in pajamas asked whether she realized that he was trying to sleep. She began to cry, and as the man closed the door, staggered hippety-hop back to the elevator, where she put on her shoe. Then she pressed the button. In a moment or two the door opened; one would have said the car was there waiting for her. She stepped in, trying to control her sobs.

Inside 1628, a man and woman looked at each other by the eerie light of a radio dial. Superficially, they were handsome: he tall, fair, big-shouldered in his evening clothes; she young, slim, lovely with her trick of throwing back her head and staring at some shadowy beyond. And yet, at closer inspection, they weren't handsome at all, or big, or lovely. There was something ferretlike about them both, something small in their faces, something wild, something a little wanton. They seemed, in some vague way, to be aware of this, and to realize that it was the reason for the intense, almost exalted delight that they took in each other, so that they touched each other eagerly, and stood close, inhaling each other's breath. Presently she said: "She's gone."

"Sounds like it."

"I've got to go, Ben."

"Oh nuts, sit down, stay a while."

"I've got to go, so she won't know. I've got to get back into my room so I can pretend it was all some kind of a mistake. I—don't want her to suffer. She's suffered enough from me."

". . . I don't want her to know either."

"Then—good night, Ben."

"Listen, did you hear what I said? I don't want her to know either. She—she's important to me. That cluck, that Swede, is stuck on her, and through her I can make him do what I want done."

"I know, I guessed all that."

"Look, you got to get this straight. She does it because—"

"She's in love with you, of course."

"And what do you say now?"

"You know what I say."

She hid her face in his coat, clung to him, dug her fingers into his arm. Obviously, they had got to a point where the word love, if either of them had uttered it, would have been somewhat inadequate. Insanity would have been better, and there was some suggestion of it as she raised her face to his. "I know, it means money. And so long as you give her her share, I don't care. I don't see how any of it could be helped. Don't worry. She won't know."

"You sure? How you going to work it?"

"I don't know . . . That's the funny thing, about what makes you bad. You can go through walls, Ben. Through walls. Once I went through a whole locker room and took four handbags and got out and I wasn't even seen. You know how I did it?"

"No."

"You never will."

He caught her in his arms, and for a few moments

148

they seemed to have melted together. Then he released her, and she floated toward the door. "Don't worry, Ben."

She was gone, and he put away the highball tray he had put out for Lefty, emptied the ashtrays, set the room to rights. In the bedroom the phone rang. "Ben?"

"Yes?"

"June."

"Oh, hello."

"I'm terribly sorry, Ben."

"About what?"

"Didn't you hear anything?"

"I've been asleep."

"Thank heaven . . . I did something terribly silly. On account of Dorothy. I—thought she was with you."

"With—*me?*"

"You don't have to snap my head off. I *admitted* it was silly. You can imagine what a ninny I felt when she popped out of the door a few minutes ago in her pajamas and all, and it was perfectly obvious she'd been asleep for hours."

"Well, it's all news to me."

"You might tell me it was a nice party."

"One thing at a time. I'm still asleep."

"Well?"

"Sure, it was swell."

"Good night, Ben."

"Good night."

He really was asleep the next time the phone rang, and he answered in a tone that was to remind June that enough was enough. But it wasn't June. It was Lefty. "Well, what do you want?"

"They got Caspar."

"You mean they rubbed him out? Who did?"

"They got him. In Mexico. They're bringing him back."

". . . Who's bringing him back?"

"The U.S. government. For income tax violation."

"How do you know? Say, what is this, anyway? What time is it? And what's the big idea calling me up at this time of morning anyhow?"

"It's five-thirty A.M., and I been passing the time with Joe Cantrell and he just had Mexico City on the long distance wire. They're flying him back today. They've left for the airport already, the planes take off at six-thirty, he'll be in Los Angeles tonight, and Lake City tomorrow. Here's where it gets good, Ben: for income tax violation, they may give him bail."

"O.K., so he gets bail."

"Just thought I'd let you know."

10

Ben saw quite a little of Dorothy the next two or three days. He gave her a key to his apartment, and would find her waiting when he came in. She was insistent, however, that they find some other place to meet. "She knows, Ben. I fooled her the other night, but now she knows. We'll have to go somewhere else. I can't bear the idea of hurting her."

But Ben's mind was on other things, particularly on the newspapers, which were reporting minutely the movements of Mr. Caspar. They carried his arrival at Mexicali, at Los Angeles, at St. Louis. At this point reporters from the Lake City papers met his plane, and rode with him on the Prairie Central to the local airport, interviewing him on the way, and giving copious space to his remarks. The general sense of them was that he had been crossed, but that he believed in being a good sport and taking it until his turn came again. At the big pictures of him, wearing the charro hat with bells on the brim that he had bought in Mexico City, Ben waxed thoughtful, and read the caption carefully, to make sure they had really been taken at the Post Office Building, in connection with the rites of booking, fingerprinting, and incarceration.

That night, with Mr. Cantrell, the new and highly praised Chief of Police, he visited his attorney, Mr. Yates, the former partner of Mr. Bleeker, the city prosecutor. He and Mr. Cantrell arrived first, and tramped the halls of the Coolidge Building for some time before Mr. Yates pattered up, opened his office, and motioned to them. Inside, he turned on the desk light and began his report. "Well, I just left Ollie Bleeker, and we spent most of the afternoon on it, and I think now I can tell you how it's going to break. Hovey Dunne, the United States Attorney, wasn't there, but we had it out with him over the telephone and I'm sure we know what he's going to do."

Mr. Cantrell fidgeted. "O.K., get to it."

"Caspar hasn't got a chance. In the first place, they've got him on so many violations of the tax law that barring slip-ups he'll be ten years serving his time."

"It's slip-ups we're worrying about."

"Chief, there can't be any slip-ups, really. The only conceivable one is that they would make a deal. The Federal people, I mean. That some sort of deal would be made for payment of those taxes, whereby they'd agree not to prosecute. But where does that get him? Your warrant is on file over there, and before they release him they've got to turn him over to you. Then he goes on trial for murder. This was a simple case of who caught him first, the city police or the Feds. Well, they've got him, that's all."

"Why don't they turn him over to us?"

"With their own charges untried?"

"Our charge is a capital offense."

"What difference does it make?"

"Plenty of difference, Yates. O.K., he serves ten years. He goes to Alcatraz, and he serves ten years. What then?"

"Then the State tries him for murder."

"And convicts him, I suppose. A fat chance! After ten years, you couldn't convict *Hitler* of murder. The witnesses have skipped, or died, or been seen, and besides the jury thinks if he served ten years he's been punished enough. The way you fixed it, after ten years he's out and it's bad."

"I didn't fix it."

"I'll say you didn't."

"He could be acquitted of murder, even now."

"O.K., then I got another murder. I got a million of them, and if the jury still won't say murder, I got a little larceny and maybe a couple of mayhems and assaults with deadly weapons. *Then,* if he's still acquitted, we got the Federal stuff to fall back on. But—get this, Yates—on murder he could burn. I don't say would, I only say could. But he'd have a good outside chance, and if that crook ever squatted hot, that would be doing something for the country."

"And you, I imagine."

"That's right."

"Not, I'm happy to say, for me."

"Yeah, even you."

As Mr. Yates looked up in surprise, Mr. Cantrell gave a short, harsh laugh. "You're right on the payroll of Ben's little outfit, his cute association that stole its machines from Caspar, and if you think Solly's going to be careful about it, and check it all up, to make sure you were told and all, why, you're flattering him quite a lot. He's not that conscientious. You're on the spot, right now."

"You mean—they're the same old machines?"

"Sure, don't you recognize them?"

"Chief, I had no idea of this."

"Yates, you're a liar."

Mr. Cantrell, after vainly pressing Mr. Yates for some other arrangement, was quite gloomy as they went out on the street, but Ben on the whole seemed relieved. He followed with interest the announcement, made late one afternoon, that Caspar had left the Post Office Building in company with F.B.I. agents, to lead them to the place he had hidden his bonds, so that he could make some sort of payment on the taxes that he owed. It was while he was dialing Mr. Cantrell, after dinner that night, to find out how this monkeyshine had turned out, that the house phone rang in the bedroom, and he went in to answer. "Ben?"

"Speaking."

"Dorothy."

"Come on up."

"I'm not in the hotel. Ben, I have another place."

"Yeah? Where is it?"

"You've been to June's old apartment?"

"Sure, I was there once or twice."

"I got the key for it today."

"You there now?"

"No. The phone's disconnected. I'm at the drug store."

"I don't like it."

"Why not?"

154

"It's hers, for one thing."

"There's not one single thing of hers in it. She's taken everything out, and there's nothing in it but the regular furniture. Besides, she only has it until January 1, and that's only two or three days off, and so far as she's concerned she's forgotten about it. I mean, she's out."

"Oh, come on over."

"Ben, I hate it there. I hear her out there, pounding on the door and crying. Ben, come on over, so I can put my arms around you in peace."

"Say, you sound friendly."

"I'll be waiting."

"O.K."

Her arms indeed went around him when he came in, and they stood for some moments in the shabby little foyer, holding each other tight, before they moved over to the sofa, and she snuggled into his arms, and they relaxed. "How in the world, Dorothy, did you find out about this place, anyway?"

"Through a friend of mine."

"Who's that?"

"Hal. Don't you know him?"

"Not by that name."

"He's a bellboy over at the hotel. He's on the late shift, the one that runs the elevator and gets you ice and does whatever you want done."

"How did *he* know about it?"

"June sent him over here, to bring her things back. He made several trips at one time and another. He even had a key, that he forgot to give back to her. So—he lent it to me. For a consideration. For five dollars. Give me five dollars."

He fished out five dollars, folded it neatly, handed

it over to her. She nodded, twisted her mouth kitten-ishly, dropped it into the neck of her dress. Then all the breath left her body, and a look of horror appeared on her face. For a second or two he talked to her, try-ing to find out what the trouble was. Then his blood turned to whey. The closet door was open, and Mr. Salvatore Gasparro, alias Solly Caspar, was standing there looking at them. "H'y, Benny."

"Hello, Sol."

Sol came over, sat down in the small battered arm chair, lit a cigar. "Sure, Hal's a friend of mine, too. Great kid. Don't you remember him, Ben?"

"Not right now I don't."

"He run a poolroom for me, quite a while back. That was the trouble with you, Ben. You thought you was too good for your work. You was always high-hatting my organization."

"I'm sorry, Sol."

"It's O.K."

Benignly Sol puffed out smoke before he went on: "It don't really make no difference any more, because I'm going to kill you, Ben. Fact of the matter that's what I want to talk about. I'm going to kill you, then I'm going to kind of amuse myself with her."

It was perhaps five feet from Ben's feet to Sol's feet, and mentally Ben measured the distance, so as to be accurate with the feint, the spring, and the blow. But Sol was telepathic in these matters. An automatic ap-peared in his hand, and he told Ben to keep his eyes front and his hands in sight. Then, laying the cigar in an ashtray, he said: "Sister, you move over here to one side, so I can keep an eye on you while I'm killing Ben." Dorothy, as if in a trance, moved as directed, and obeyed when he told her to sit down in the wooden chair that stood against the wall. Ben, at a command, stood up. "That's good, Ben, just like you are now. Now I want you to walk backwards, slow so you don't stumble over nothing, and when you get to the bathroom I'll tell you to stop and you stop. Then you feel around back of you for the knob and open the door. Then when I tell you to start moving again I want you to back in there and climb in the tub and lay down. I'm going to kill you in the tub, so I can close the door and not hear no blood dripping while I'm playing around with her. I don't like to hear blood. And besides, when I shoot in the bathroom they're not so liable to hear it outside. You ready?"

". . . I guess so, Sol."

"Then get going!"

Slowly, on jerky, shaking legs Ben began backing toward the bathroom. Slowly, his eyes fixed in a marble stare, his lips parted in a dreadful grin, the gun held in one hand while the other steadied it, Sol followed. He followed with a sort of creep, and whispered as he came, filthy, obscene things about Dorothy. When Ben reached the door, Sol breathed the command to halt, and Ben fumbled for the knob. Presently he found it, opened the door, resumed his backward progress. Sol resumed his creep.

In the bathroom, Sol became less cautious with his voice, and screamed at Ben, with appropriate curses, to get in the tub and lie down, and be quick about it. Sol was framed in the doorway, and Ben, in the dark bathroom, moved to obey. Then the place filled with light, and with the crash of a gun. Ben staggered, whimpered, clutched his belly. Then, to his astonishment, Caspar curled up and rolled over on his side.

He stepped over Caspar into the living room. She

was still sitting there, a gun in her lap, staring at the body, her face lovely. When she looked up her eyes were dancing, as though the two bright points of light in them were controlled by an electric switch. "I've always carried it. I've carried it since I was fifteen years old. In my handbag. This is the first time I've used it."

"O.K."

"I didn't miss."

"We got work to do, but one thing first."

"Yes, Ben."

"I'm nuts about you. You're the first woman I ever cared about, and you'll be the last. I'm nuts about you, and I want to tell you so. Now. While he's still warm."

"I love you, Ben."

"O.K., that's what I mean."

"I meant to kill him, and I did. Who was he?"

"A gangster."

"He's dead."

"Yes."

Suddenly himself again, Ben stooped down and kissed her, and went into the bathroom to look. Caspar was lying as he had fallen, looking small and queer.

"You got a mirror?"

"Yes, right here."

He held the little mirror she gave him in front of Sol's mouth, then in front of his nostrils. Nodding grimly, he handed the mirror back. Striding again into the living room, he took a quick look around. Sol's hat and coat he found in the closet, and carefully laid them on a chair. The cigar, still burning in the ashtray, he got rid of in the bathroom. "The next question is, how did he get here?"

"How do you mean, Ben?"

"Did he come alone?"

"Oh my, is there somebody waiting for him?"

"I don't think so. I've known this bird from way back. This is the celebrated Mr. Caspar you've been reading about in the newspapers, *if* you've been reading them. How he made his break from the Feds I don't know, but he wouldn't be taking anybody along, on a job like this, not even that bellboy. If it was somebody he could trust, he'd have had them knock me off in the first place. So—"

"What do we do with him? I'm known to be here."

"You mind waiting here a few minutes?"

"I'm not afraid, if that's what you mean."

"O.K., I'll tap three times when I get back."

"How long will you be?"

"Not long. Better turn out the lights."

"All right."

They turned out all lights, and he studied every window that looked down on the rear areaway. Then he tiptoed to the door, peeped out. Then, running lightly down the stairs, he emerged on the street, turned, and walked briskly away. As he went his eyes kept shooting from right to left. He had gone but a few steps past his own car before he came to what he was half hoping to find. It was Sol's old familiar armored car, that he had driven a thousand times, parked just above the little apartment house. He didn't stop by it, however. He walked past, staring at every tree, every car.

Then he quickly crossed the street and came down, doing the same thing on the other side. He couldn't be sure whether Sol had slipped into the storage shed back of the Columbus and got the car himself, or had phoned somebody to bring it around. He was taking no chances that a pair of eyes were on him somewhere, watching what he did.

The street, however, was deserted. He crossed over to the car, found it locked. Taking his keys from his pocket, he fingered them, found the one he had used daily, before, when he was driving for Sol. He unlocked the car, got in, put the key in the ignition. Starting, he threw on the lights and rolled silently down to the corner. This was a little neighborhood boulevard, and he was cautious about turning into it. He drove the half block beside the apartment house, then turned into the alley behind it, cutting his lights as he did so. He drove to the entrance of the rear areaway, stopped within a few inches of it, set his brake, got out without slamming the door. Then he hurried around to the front of the apartment house again, ran up the stairs, tapped on the door. Dorothy let him in. "O.K., now we got a chance."

Rapidly, in whispers, he explained what they had to do. Soon, in the areaway below, a girl stood motionless, watching. There was a sound of something heavy, dropping. She scanned the windows. When no face appeared, she gave a little cough. From the shadows a man came staggering under a heavy load. When he reached the alley, and no face appeared at a window, the girl flitted after him. Reaching the car, she jumped in and helped him wrestle his burden to the floor space in front of the back seat. Then she got out and disappeared. The man got in, backed into the street, put on his lights, waited. Soon another car came around the corner, stopped, winked its lights. The man winked his lights. Then he started, and the other car started, and this tandem procession wound its way through the streets of the city until it came to a short street, quite deserted, in the downtown shopping center. Here the man pulled over and stopped. Then he snapped down all locks. Then he took his keys. Then he got out and slammed everything shut. Then he walked back to the other car, which was just now coming to a stop. Then he got in and the girl at the wheel drove off.

"What now, Ben?"
"Alibi. Where did you tell June you were going?"
"Picture show."
"Then you'd better go to one. Get a program. Talk to an usher, or the manager, or somebody, to establish the date—"
"I know."
"Here's a buck."
"I love this car."
"It's yours."
"You mean it?"
"Yes."
". . . You're mine, too."
"O.K."

II

For two days Ben and Dorothy took turns walking past the car on the downtown street, at hourly, and even half-hourly intervals. It remained there exactly as they had left it, until they thought they would go insane.

The newspapers shrieked the story of Caspar's escape from the officers. They told how he had brought them to the Columbus, on the assurance that his wealth was stored in a vault there; how he had led them to a room, sat them down, and spun a knob in the wall; how a panel had then opened, and how he had stepped through it, while the officers watched; how the panel had rolled into place behind him, and they had sat there for a full minute before waking up to what had happened; how they had then spent the next ten minutes making their escape from a locked room, via the cornice that ran around the building; how Caspar had appeared in the lobby and calmly greeted his friends; how he had sauntered back to the storage garage, got into his armored car, lit a cigar, commented that it looked like snow, driven out to the street, and vanished.

Details of the man-hunt that had been organized to capture him were published in succeeding editions. It was, according to the *Pioneer,* at least, the first man-hunt ever undertaken on a hemispherical scale, since all plane lines that ran north to Canada, or south to Mexico and Latin America, had agreed to cooperate. And all the time Sol's metal coffin stood in view of thousands of people, looking like every other car on the street, smart, streamlined, shiny.

On New Year's Eve, June came up for an afternoon visit, and Ben talked pleasantly of her party, her mother, even of her sister, who he said was a very nice girl. But he was nervous, and toyed with his key holder, a neat leather contraption that kept each key in its place, on a little hook. He dropped it, and it popped open. He picked it up by one key that stuck out from the others, and jiggled it back and forth, so it clinked.

"You do have so many keys, don't you?"

The jiggling missed a beat, but only one. Ben then yawned, asked her if she would have a drink. She declined, and he said he thought he would have one. He went whistling to the pantribar, reappeared at once with the announcement he would have to open another bottle. Nonchalantly, he went into the bedroom, took his hat and coat from the closet, opened the door to the hall, looked out. Then quietly he walked to the elevator, pressed the button, stood looking at the entrance door of 1628. When the car stopped he was yawning, and remarked to the operator that these holiday parties sure didn't give a guy much sleep. The operator said they sure didn't. He asked for Hal. The operator said Hal must be sick, he'd been off for a couple of days. He said yeah, he'd missed him.

"But, Ben, *how* could she know?"

"She could know from Hal. She could know by trailing you, after not believing you were going to a picture show. She could know by hearing it at the City Hall. She could know plenty different ways, but you know what I think?"

"What's that?"

"I think they found Caspar. I think they found him pretty soon, maybe that night. I think they found him and took him out and put something else under that robe, hoping we'd come back for something we forgot."

"What did we forget?"

"Do you know?"

"Nothing."

"So *we* think."

"A remark about keys is not much to go on."

"With the look in her eye, it was plenty."

"Where do we go now?"

"Honduras, maybe."

They were driving through the afternoon twilight, she at the wheel. They had taken a street that didn't quite go through the center of town, but suddenly his ear caught something, and he had her drive over to one of the main intersections. There he bought a paper, and held it up to her so she could see the great black headline: CASPAR BODY FOUND. After reading a moment or two he gave an exclamation.

"There it is."

"What is it?"

" '*It is understood the police will arrest a big local*

racketeer, prominent since the Jansen administration took office, and probably a young college girl—' "

"How *could* they?"

"Never mind. Drive."

After a few miles, however, he gave another exclamation, took out his wallet, counted the contents. "Dorothy, do you have any money?"

"Fifty cents."

"I've got nine dollars."

He stared like a sleepwalker at the road ahead. "I've got money in the bank, thousands in the bank, and I don't dare cash a check. I've got this car, and I don't dare sell it. I've been just sitting around letting the grass grow under my feet. I was so sure we'd done a bang-up job that I thought they'd never guess it. I never once remembered I'd be the first man they'd think of, whether we did a bang-up job or not. And as for you, I've been with you morning, noon, and night—"

"What are we going to do?"

"I don't know."

"We'll need gas pretty soon."

"We're O.K. on that. We got the credit card—"

"What's the matter?"

"We don't dare use it."

"It's all right. We have each other."

"We don't even dare get married."

They drove some miles through the gathering dusk, aimlessly, aware that they were going nowhere. He looked at her then, and she turned her head, and for a moment they were staring at each other.

"Dorothy, we got one chance."

"What is it, Ben?"

"One crazy chance."

"I don't care if it's crazy."

"I always carry a little notebook."

"Yes, I've noticed it."

"There's something in there I don't understand. It's a flock of numbers. I don't know how they got in there, I don't remember copying them down any time, I don't place what they are. Maybe I never knew what they are. I copy a lot of things down, just in case. But the other day, when I rented a bigger box at the bank, I tumbled to what they are. They're a safe combination."

"Yes? Go on, Ben. Hurry up."

"Caspar, he hid his dough somewhere."

"Ben, I don't think it's crazy!"

"As to where he hid it, I think I know. I kept noticing we were out Memorial Boulevard oftener than there seemed any reason for us to be. And there's that toolshed out there, right in the middle of a vacant lot, that just don't make sense. Are you game to go there with me tonight? Will you—"

"Ben, I'll simply love it."

"Got a cigarette?"

"No, I'm sorry."

It was dark when they got back to Lake City, after buying gasoline, for cash. She threaded her way through the traffic area, and he bought another paper. It was a green one, the day's final, and his picture was in it, as well as hers. He was bitter against Cantrell, for giving him no warning, and against June, who he was sure was the only one that could have furnished both pictures. She made no comment, except that June had always been good to her. They drove out Memorial, to the place where Lefty had appeared screaming the night Dick Delany had been murdered. Here they turned into the side road. Cautiously, they kept on until they came to the toolshed that he and June had noticed, the morning they started checking up. Here they stopped. He took the flashlight with which the car was provided, and they got out.

Approaching the toolshed they peeped into it, through one of its small windows. Visible were picks, shovels, a wheelbarrow, a trough for mixing mortar. "Don't look very promising."

He sounded glum, but she was staring straight in front of her nose. "This window is barred on the inside. That doesn't look like an ordinary toolshed."

Leaving him to watch for cars, she took the flashlight and made the rounds of the little building, presently calling him. Shooting the light under the roof, she pointed to a metal contrivance and asked if he knew what it was. He whistled. "I'll say I do. It's the switch of a burglar alarm, and it's exactly like the one at his beach shack, over by the lake." Reaching up, he threw the switch off. "Now I know we're getting warm."

They went around to the door now, and shot the flash at it. It was of heavy planking, and fastened with a modern lock. She stood thinking, then ran over to the car. When she came back she had a tire iron and the tow line. With the tire iron she had him force up the cheap little window. The tow cable she fastened to the bars inside. "Now when I back up you hook this on the rear axle." In a moment she was in the car, backing it unlighted into the lot, up to the shack. When she stopped he looped the cable around the axle and made it fast with the hook. She started the car. The cable tightened, then began to deliver all the incredible power of a modern automobile. The shack shook and made creaking noises. Then, to Ben's astonishment but evidently not to hers, it teetered for a moment and came crashing over on its side. She jumped out, and then stood watching to see if the noise had attracted somebody's attention. Traffic went by on Memorial as indifferently as it had before. She looked at him, excited, exultant. "I told you. I can go through walls."

Freeing the cable and putting it back in the car, so they could leave in an instant if they had to, they next gave their attention to what the shack had covered. But they no sooner shot the flash into the pile of tools now exposed to the night than she gave a little scream. He patted her arm, said it was nothing but a rat, said *scat*. Then the hair rose on his neck at what the rat had been carrying. It was a hand. Then he knew that here, some place, was all that was left of Arch Rossi, the boy who simply disappeared. She recovered before he did, and pointed to a ring in the boards. He put his finger into it, lifted, and a trapdoor came up. Under it was a hole, with a ladder leading into it, and concrete on one side. Guiding himself with the torch, he crept down the ladder, looked around. On three sides of the hole was raw earth. But on the fourth side, built into the concrete, was a steel door, and in the middle of it the shiny knob of a safe dial. "O.K., come on down."

"Somebody ought to stand guard."

"I'll need you."

"All right."

She was beside him in a few seconds. He handed her his little red book, after finding a page and turning it down. "Read me those numbers, one at a time, then soon as you read one, shoot the light on the dial."

"R six."

"Right six it is."

"L twenty-two."

"Left twenty-two."

There were six numbers in all, and as she read them he manipulated the dial. After the last spin, there came a faint click and he pulled. The door swung open and he grabbed the flash, shooting it inside. Visible were several large canvas sacks. "Ha, he had the right idea, but they were too fast for him, just like they were for me. O.K. Now I'm going to climb halfway up the ladder and you hand me the sacks. Set the light on the floor, up-ended."

She could drag the sacks out of the vault but she couldn't lift them, and he had to come clear down the ladder, shoulder one, creep up, and buck it out onto the grass. Even so, it was only a few minutes before they were all out of the hole and in the car. He piled them on the floor of the coupe, so there was hardly room for his legs, and she took the wheel, and they scooted. He slid the clasps, got a sack open. "What is it, Ben?"

"I don't know, looks like bonds."

"They can be sold, can't they?"

"I think so."

He got another sack open, gave a quick, startled cry. "Dorothy! It's money! It's dough! Fives! *Packs and packs and packs of them.*"

"Oh my, let me see."

"Look."

"And tens, Ben—and twenties!"

"Now, thank God, we got a chance."

"In twenty four hours, by taking turns driving, we can be in Mexico. We won't get any sleep, but we can do it."

". . . Mexico's out."

"We can't stay here."

"We're going to Canada. We're going to Canada, and we're going to join up for the war. Maybe we got to use other names, but we're going to join up. Then, when it's over, we can settle there, or somewhere. We'll have all the dough we need. And if we do get caught and brought back, we still got a chance. If you went in the war, you always got a chance."

"Will they take you?"

"You mean this hernia? That can be fixed. It's a simple operation. It takes ten days."

"Why the war, Ben? The real why, I mean."

"I want to. I want to do something I'm not ashamed of."

"It's not to get rid of me?"

"Didn't you hear me? You're going to join up too. If we work it right, we can get into outfits that'll let us see a lot of each other. Then when we got it lined up, we can get married. Even if it's under phoney names, *we'll* know it's legal."

"Then I want to, too. Kiss me, Ben."

". . . I got to have a smoke."

"Me too. Here's a store. You hop off and get some, three or four packs, and I'll drive around the block."

He went into the drug store, bought four packages of cigarettes, dropped three of them into his overcoat pocket. Then he went outside, clawing the fourth package open with trembling fingers. Then he looked up and saw it happen, a perfect slow movie: her approach to the curb, just a few feet from the drug store; her obvious failure to see the fireplug; the toot of the traffic officer's whistle, and his slow, angry cross to the car; his comments to Dorothy, heated, no doubt, by the peevishness that comes from directing New Year's Eve traffic. For some seconds Ben stood, so close he could

170

hear what the officer said. Then, all of a sudden the officer stopped, stared hard at Dorothy. By that Ben knew he recognized her from the picture in the paper. He started over, with some idea of getting close, of using some football trick, of disabling the officer somehow, so they could make their getaway with all the money in the world.

When the officer looked up he recognized him, too, and drew his gun. Ben opened his mouth to tell him to go easy with it, but he probably didn't picture to himself the size of his shoulders, the ominous resolution of his approach. The officer fired, and he felt a terrifying impact.

12

For the second consecutive day, Ben stared at Mr. Cantrell with calm, baleful malevolence, and insulted him. Less bitterly, he insulted Mr. Bleeker, the prosecutor, who sat across from Dr. Ronde, the young interne, and Miss Houston, the rather pretty nurse. Mr. Bleeker let Mr. Cantrell do the talking this time, advisedly, perhaps, because he had let his temper run away with him yesterday, and made things difficult. Mr. Cantrell began with the statement that they had news today. The girl, Dorothy Lyons, had practically confessed, and her gun had been found. Also, evidence had been found in the bathroom of her sister's apartment, quite a few things of interest. Also, the sacks of money had furnished a motive. To all this, Ben replied that Mr. Cantrell was a dirty liar; that both he and Mr. Bleeker were a pair of heels to boot, as they had been on his payroll, and now they had turned on him. To this, Mr. Cantrell returned a grin and the assurance that Ben didn't mean it. And just as a friend, he added that he wished Ben would make a clean breast of the whole thing, agree to a plea, and then be left in peace to regain his strength. For his own part, he wouldn't be surprised if Ben would be let off with a suspended sentence, especially in view of what the girl had to say.

To this, Ben replied that he wouldn't be surprised that Mr. Cantrell had had something to do with the death of Arch Rossi, and that he had better look out, now that the body had been found. Dr. Ronde protested against the whole proceeding, saying that every minute it lasted was just that much more drain on the patient's vitality, and declining to be responsible for what might happen if it kept up.

When they were gone, Ben lay back wearily on the pillow and said to the uniformed patrolman who sat in the corner reading magazines: "Why can't they let you alone? When they see you're not going to talk, what's the idea of coming in here and just hammering at you."

"Oh, you'll talk."

"I don't think you know me."

"I don't think you know what you got."

"What did you say?"

"Peritonitis, Grace. Oh, they sewed up all those holes in your intestines, and it don't hurt any, we all know that. I got shot once, myself. But that's just the start of it. After that comes the peritonitis, and then your temp goes up. It's 101 now, see? It'll go to 104, and maybe 105. O.K., the higher it goes the more you can't keep your mouth shut. You get wacky enough, you'll spill it, and the police department stenographer, he's right outside."

"I get it now."

"She killed him, didn't she?"

"I got nothing to say."

"O.K."

The nurse brought an ice pack, and around noon Lefty came in. Ben motioned him over, and they went into a long, whispered consultation, while the officer read his magazine. Lefty departed, and the nurse brought more ice.

The long afternoon wore on, with Ben fighting his tongue, trying to make it shut up. Presently he asked: "What time is it?"

"Four-thirty-five."

"O.K., I'm ready to talk."

"What?"

"Didn't you hear me?"

"O.K. I'll get the stenographer."

"Hey, wait a minute, not so fast. The pothook guy, he's all right, but I'm not telling it here. I got my own ideas on it."

"What do you mean, you're not telling it here?"

"I'm telling it at Caspar's shack."

"What shack?"

"His shack by the lake, stupid."

"Why?"

"Because there's where it happened."

"Hey, what is this?"

"I tell you I'm ready to talk, and I demand to be taken out where the crime was committed so I can show you and not waste any more juice than I have to. You heard what the doctor said. If I keep this up I'm going to die. You got to take me out to that shack. You got to have this girl there, Dorothy Lyons, and I want her sister there, and my lawyer, Yates. And I want Lefty there. You don't have to do anything about him.

174

He's coming here and riding out with me. He's bringing some stuff I'll want to show you."

This strange harangue brought Cantrell over a half hour later, more than skeptical. He was qiute sure, he said, that the crime had been committed in the sister's apartment. Then why this nonsense about going to the shack? "It's O.K. by me if we don't go there, Joe. You want me to talk and I'm willing, on my own terms. Well, nuts, if you don't think we were there go have a look at the cigarettes we were smoking while we sat around waiting. And our candle, stuck to the floor."

At this allusion to the visits Ben and June had paid to the shack, away back in the spring, Mr. Cantrell's eyes narrowed, and for a moment Ben feared the police had already been there, and noted the cigarettes. However, Mr. Cantrell, if not convinced, at least was sure that something was brewing, probably worth the trip.

"O.K., Ben."

"They've got to be there. All of them."

"No trouble about it. Take it easy."

"Lefty's coming here."

"We'll take him."

It was thought advisable to wait until after dinner though, and it was nearly eight o'clock when a strange company began to gather at the snow-powdered beach shack of the late Mr. Caspar. First came Mr. Cantrell, who put the lights on, and with his uniformed department chauffeur, began poking around with some interest. Then came Mr. Bleeker, shivering and asking if they couldn't have a little heat. Mr. Cantrell shook his head. Heat would be pleasant, but some of the evidence promised by Grace had already been found in the fireplace, and as there was no way of knowing what was coming, the case could not be jeopardized by starting a fire that might burn important items up. So far, he said, blowing on his hands with his steaming breath, it looked as though there were angles not uncovered yet. Possibly, he conjectured there was some connection between what went on here at the shack and what went on in the vault.

Mrs. Caspar arrived, in deep mourning, with a woman companion. Mr. Cantrell received her courteously, apologized for the cold, but said it could not be helped. Dorothy and June arrived, with police matrons. There was a wait, while everybody shivered, and then the ambulance siren was heard outside. Ben, on a stretcher, was carried in by two orderlies, with Dr. Ronde and Mr. Yates, and Lefty following along behind. "Where you want him, Doc?"

"Right here on the sofa, I think."

"Easy with him."

"Lay the stretcher right on it. Keep him covered!"

During this operation Ben stared at the orderlies, nodded when Mr. Cantrell asked if he was comfortable. Mr. Cantrell then launched into a speech. He said that Ben had put everybody to a lot of trouble, and he hoped he would make it as short and simple as he could, as it was cold, and they were all anxious to get some place where it was more comfortable. Was he ready? Ben, speaking clearly, said he was, and Mr. Cantrell motioned the various police functionaries who were stationed near the door to step forward. The stenographers sat down, put their notebooks on their knees. The guards stood against the wall. "O.K.," said Mr. Cantrell.

Ben closed his eyes, and one finger appeared from

under the covers. It almost looked like some sort of weak, delirious signal.

"Do you, Ben, take this woman, Dorothy, to be thy wedded wife, to love and cherish, for better or for worse?"

There was a stir, and nobody looked into the shadows more astonished than Dorothy, as she tried to see where the voice was coming from. Yet as soon as Ben said "I do" it resumed:

"Do you, Dorothy, take this man, Ben, to be thy wedded husband, to love and cherish, for better or for worse?"

Quick comprehension lighted her face, then, and she replied, "I do," quickly, breathlessly.

The voice went on: *"I pronounce you—"*

Mr. Cantrell leaped and caught Lefty behind the ear with a right hook that sent him to the floor. Lefty jumped up, and for one second was the killer who had served time in more prisons than he could quite remember. Then he backed away from Mr. Cantrell, who had already drawn a gun. "Oh, no, you don't, Joe. You don't shoot me, because I haven't signed that marriage certificate yet. And when I sign it, it's legal, boy. I got a preacher's license, and the marriage license was issued in the Quartz Courthouse at four-thirty this afternoon, one minute before they closed. It's a county license, and we're in the county. That's why we came out here. . . . *I pronounce them man and wife, Joe."*

Looking up at Mr. Cantrell, his cheeks red, his eyes bright, Ben said, "Now try to make me talk against her, you rat."

"And try to make *me* talk."

Dorothy went over, knelt down, and put her arms

around Ben. Almost at once she looked at him sharply. "My, but your face is hot."

Dr. Ronde, who had been stalking disapprovingly in the shadows, turned quickly, came over. He put his hand under the covers, felt Ben's abdomen. Then he barked a command at his orderlies.

An hour and a half later, patrolmen with red flashlights stood in the bushes, waving at a coroner, who drove a sedan, and an undertaker, who drove a light truck. At one side stood two women. One of them, small and dark, sobbed jerkily. The other stared unhearing into the night. For once her eyes did not dance, and for once she attained a great sombre beauty.

ABOUT THE AUTHOR

JAMES M. CAIN (1892–1977) is recognized today as one of the masters of the hard-boiled school of American novels. Born in Baltimore, the son of the president of Washington College, he began his career as reporter on the Baltimore papers, served in the American Expeditionary Force in World War I and wrote the material for *The Cross of Lorraine,* the newspaper of the 79th Division. He returned to become professor of journalism at St. John's College in Annapolis and then worked for H. L. Mencken on *The American Mercury.* He later wrote editorials for Walter Lippmann on the *New York World* and was for a short period managing editor of *The New Yorker,* before he went to Hollywood as a script writer. His first novel, *The Postman Always Rings Twice,* was published when he was forty-two and at once became a sensation. It was tried for obscenity in Boston, was said by Albert Camus to have inspired his own book, *The Stranger,* and is now a classic. Cain followed it the next year with *Double Indemnity,* leading Ross Macdonald to write years later, "Cain has won unfading laurels with a pair of native American masterpieces, *Postman* and *Double Indemnity,* back to back." Cain published eighteen books in all and was working on his autobiography at the time of his death.

VINTAGE MYSTERIES